For Joe Geisler
For being part of our family,
For being a terrific father.
Love, Mary Anne

Books by Mary Anne Wilson

HARLEQUIN AMERICAN ROMANCE

*Just for Kids
†Return to Silver Creek

"How could I have destroyed your life?" Cain wanted to know

Holly would have stood, but he was right there, and any move she made would have propelled her straight into him. She didn't want to touch him, not now. "Please, this is ridiculous" was all she told him, sure she sounded as panicked as she felt. "I just need to go. Forget that I said anything. It doesn't matter, not at all. Not anymore."

"You bet it does," he said, the harshness in his words almost making her flinch. "You know, all my life people have accused me of things that they thought I did. From the start. Back at the orphanage. Right on through the rest of my life." His eyes narrowed as he looked at her. "I hate the idea of you doing that, too. I really hate it."

She did flinch at that. She heard her own voice, but it sounded distant and odd.

"Then we're even, aren't we?"

Dear Reader,

Cain Stone has always been a gambler and a risk taker. But when he goes home to Silver Creek and meets single mother Holly Winston, he realizes from the start that the gamble he takes getting close to her and her tiny daughter has higher odds than anything he's ever known.

Holly isn't into taking chances. She's tried it and paid for it. At this stage in her life, opening her heart to anyone is a risk she won't take—until Cain Stone walks into her neatly arranged world.

I've always been intrigued by the concept of opposites attracting, and when the stakes are high, this is even more compelling. In *Holiday Homecoming,* the third installment in my RETURN TO SILVER CREEK four-book series, opposites not only attract, they find themselves in a world neither has entered before. It's all about love and all about trust, the very elements that neither has experienced.

I hope you enjoy the journey of Holly and Cain as they find each other and each takes the biggest gamble of their life.

Don't miss the fourth installment in the RETURN TO SILVER CREEK series, when Jack Prescott finds his own way home to Silver Creek.

Holiday Homecoming

Mary Anne Wilson

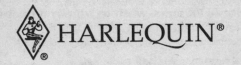

HARLEQUIN®

TORONTO • NEW YORK • LONDON
AMSTERDAM • PARIS • SYDNEY • HAMBURG
STOCKHOLM • ATHENS • TOKYO • MILAN • MADRID
PRAGUE • WARSAW • BUDAPEST • AUCKLAND

ISBN 0-373-75096-X

HOLIDAY HOMECOMING

Copyright © 2005 by Mary Anne Wilson.

www.eHarlequin.com

Printed in U.S.A.

Prologue

Las Vegas, Nevada
One month earlier

"I'm not going back to Silver Creek," Cain Stone said. "I don't have the time—or the inclination to make the time. Besides, it's not my home."

The man he was talking to, Jack Prescott, shook his head, then motioned with both hands at Caine's sterile penthouse. It was done in black and white—black marble floors, white stone fireplace, white leather furniture. The only splash of color came from the sofa pillows, which were various shades of red. "And this is?"

The Dream Catcher Hotel and Casino on the Strip in Las Vegas was a place to be. The place Cain worked. The part of the world that he owned. His place. But his home? No. He'd never had one. "It's my place," he said honestly.

Jack, an angular man, with almost shoulder-length dark hair peppered with gray, who was dressed as usual in faded jeans, an open-necked navy shirt and his well-worn leather boots, leaned back in the semicircular couch to face the bank of windows that looked down on the city sprawling twenty stories below. "Cain, come on. You haven't been back in years, and it's the holidays."

"Bah, humbug," Cain said with a slight smile, wishing that the feeble joke would ease the growing tension in him. A tension that had started when Jack had first asked him to return to Silver Creek. "You know that for people like us there are no holidays. They're the heavy times in the year. I look forward to Christmas the way Ebenezer did. You get through it and make as much money as you can."

Jack didn't respond with any semblance of a smile. Instead, he muttered, "God, you're cynical."

"Realistic," Cain amended with a shrug. "But is it so important to you that I go to Silver Creek now?"

"Like I said, it's the holidays, and that means friends. Josh is there, and Gordie, who's at his clinic twenty-four hours a day. We can get drunk, ski down Main Street or take on Killer Run again. Whatever you want."

Jack, Josh and Gordie were as close to a family as Cain had had as a child. The orphanage hadn't been anything out of Dickens, but it hadn't been family. His three friends were. The four of them had done everything together, including getting into trouble and wiping out on Killer Run. "Tempting," Cain said, a pure lie at that moment. "But no deal."

"I won't stop asking," Jack said.

Cain stood and crossed to the built-in bar by the bank of windows. He ignored the alcohol and glasses and picked up a pack of unopened cards, one of several. He caught a glimpse of himself in the mirrors behind the bar before he turned to Jack. He was tall, about Jack's height at six foot one or so, with dark hair worn a bit long like Jack's, and brushed by gray like Jack's. His eyes, though, were deep blue, in contrast to Jack's, which were almost black.

Cain was sure he could match Jack dollar for dollar if he had to, and just as Jack didn't look like the richest man in Silver Creek, Cain didn't fit the image of a wealthy hotel-casino owner in Las Vegas. Few owners dressed in Levi's and T-shirts; even fewer went without any jewelry, including a watch. He had a closet full of expensive suits and silk shirts, but he hardly ever wore them. Still, he fit in at the Dream Catcher Hotel and Casino. It was about the only place he'd ever fit in. He didn't fit in Silver Creek. He never had.

He went back to Jack with the cards, broke the seal on the deck, and as he slipped the cards out of the package, he said, "Let's settle this once and for all."

"I'm not going to play poker with you," Jack told him. "I don't stand a chance."

Cain eyed his friend as he sat by him on the couch. "We'll keep it simple," he murmured. He took the cards out of the box, tossed the empty box on the onyx coffee table in front of them and shuffled the deck. "We'll cut for it. I'll even let you pick high or low to win."

"What's at stake?" Jack asked.

"If you win, I'll head north to Silver Creek for a few days around the holidays."

Jack took the deck when Cain offered it to him. He shuffled the cards again, then put them facedown on the coffee table. But he didn't cut them. He cast Cain a sideways glance. "How much time does this cover—your not returning to Silver Creek?"

"Forever, or until I decide that I want to go back."

Jack hesitated. He wasn't a gambler like Cain. He'd been born to money. Cain had been born to nothing, and finally had something. Cain was used to gambling in every sense of the word. And he was used to winning. "High card wins?" Jack finally said.

Cain nodded.

"Okay." Jack picked up a third of the deck and turned the bottom card up so they could both see it. An ace of hearts. Usually the best card in the deck. But not for Cain this time. "Two out of three?" he suggested.

Jack laughed. "Hell, no, I'm standing pat."

Cain sat back, raking his fingers through his dark hair with a rough sigh. "I thought you would."

Jack stood and reached for his suede jacket. "When will you be home?" he asked.

Cain glanced up at him. He wouldn't argue with Jack about where home was. Instead, he spoke truthfully. "I've got a lot to do here. I'll call you and tell you."

Jack didn't move. "When?" he repeated.

Cain held up both hands, palms out to Jack in surrender. "Okay, okay, let me check my calendar."

"Oh, sure, what calendar? You sleep, you work, you eat. Take out the work part, and you can eat and sleep in Silver Creek." He grinned. "And we've got the best snow this year. The skiing is fantastic."

Cain never skied anymore. Once the sport had been his lifeline. He'd sneak out of the orphanage and head for the mountain to Killer Run—the Killer, as they'd called it. At dawn it had been all his, and he'd savored the freedom of it. "Did you ever get the land with the Killer on it from Old Man Jennings?" he asked, remembering that some time ago Jack had said he wanted to include the run in the runs at the resort, for advanced skiers.

Jack shook his head. "No, the old man's as stubborn in

death as he was when he was alive. His heir doesn't want to part with it." He smiled slightly as he shrugged into his jacket. "But I can change that."

Cain stood to face Jack. "I'm sure you will," he said. "Okay, I'll be up sometime between Thanksgiving and New Year's."

Jack clapped a hand on his shoulder. "I'm holding you to it, Cain. I'll tell Joshua and Gordie and the four of us will be together for a few days."

"You do that," he murmured as he walked with Jack to the elevator.

Jack turned back to Cain as the elevator door opened. "I can't wait," he said, and got into the car.

Cain didn't move until the door had slid shut behind Jack, then he headed for his office off the living area. He'd figure how to get out of going back to Silver Creek later, but right now, he had work that wouldn't keep.

He didn't make it to the office before the phone sitting on the black enamel table behind the couch rang. He reached for it, glanced at the caller ID and recognized the cell phone number on the readout. "Jack?" he said as he answered it.

Jack didn't hesitate. "Stop thinking about ways to get out of this bet. You can come up before Christmas. I'll reserve a cabin for you from the twelfth with an open departure date."

"You've thought of everything."

"Don't mention it," Jack said, and hung up.

Cain put the phone back and kept going to his office. He dropped into the black leather chair behind his glass-topped desk in the book-lined room and stared down at the Strip.

Going back. He exhaled, and speculated he should have stacked the cards. Anything not to be in the position he was now in. He'd have to go back to Silver Creek, stay a few days, then leave. But he knew with a certainty that after he left, he'd never go back to Silver Creek again.

Chapter One

Cain returned to Silver Creek exactly one week before Christmas. He drove through the massive stone-pillar gates of the Inn at Silver Creek and wended his way up the brick drive, banked on either side with plowed snow. He went toward the main lodge, a meandering building that ran north-south and changed in height from three stories to one, then to two and back to three. Against the backdrop of snow, the wood-and-stone structure looked determinedly rustic. No, it looked like a rich man's version of rustic, from the stained glass windows that rivaled those of Italian cathedrals, to the massive stone chimneys puffing smoke into the late-afternoon air.

He drove past the main entrance and valet parking and headed to the far end of the lodge, which rose three stories into the darkening skies. He pulled his new SUV into a slot marked Private and stopped, then pushed the door. A blast of frigid air hit him as he stepped onto the cleared cobbled pavement. He'd made good on the payment for his bet. He was in Silver Creek. He'd stay for a few days, maybe leave after two, if he could work it out. He'd play things by ear.

He hunched into the chilling wind that whipped off the towering Sierra Nevada, which framed the town on the east and west, and stuffed his hands into the pockets of his black leather bomber jacket. He looked around at the grounds of the Inn at Silver Creek—Jack's project that had been going on forever. A posh, expensive, very private ski resort for the rich and sometimes famous or infamous, built on land that Jack's family had owned since the founding of the town.

The resort now sprawled over acres and acres of mountain terrain, offering secluded cabins for those who could afford them and promising the most precious commodity money could buy: privacy. The main building contained suites, gathering rooms and two separate restaurants, with enough luxury to satisfy the most discriminating guest.

Cain turned to the lodge and took the cleared steps to the door marked Private. Without warning, the door opened and a young guy in slouchy snow gear rushed out. "Sorry, dude," the guy muttered as he barely avoided a collision with Cain. Then, with a "Merry Christmas!" tossed over his shoulder, he jumped down the steps and loped toward the main trail that led to the scattered private lodges.

"Bah, humbug," Cain breathed roughly.

He stepped inside, into a wide hallway with stone floors, aged wooden walls in a deep cherrywood polished to a mellow glow and the sense of luxury—from the Persian rug runners to the paintings on the wall, which had their own security system to protect them. Christmas music was piped in, and someone had discreetly nestled small twinkling lights in the crown molding between the wood of the wall and the beamed ceiling.

He never had been comfortable with wealthy trappings, even at the casino, and at this time of year, the extras for the holidays made his discomfort even worse. He suspected that was why he kept his penthouse sparsely furnished, without any great works of art or any antiques. There wasn't a trace of gold in the place or a trace of Christmas. You could take the orphan out of the orphanage, but you couldn't take the orphanage out of the orphan, he mused as he undid his jacket and headed toward a barely visible door in the paneling to his left.

He hit a button that exposed a security number panel, put in the code, then stood back, waiting for the elevator. He didn't want to be here, but he'd see his friends, then he'd leave. For good. He couldn't think of one reason to come back here again.

The elevator went directly to Jack's living quarters on the third floor, and when the door finally slid open for Cain to get into the elevator, he wasn't expecting to encounter anyone. If he had, he would have expected it to be with Jack, or possibly Jack's second-in-command, a huge man named Malone.

Instead, Cain came face-to-face with a woman. She was tiny, barely five feet in height, he'd guess, almost drowning in a heavy navy jacket, jeans and huge snow boots. Fiery auburn hair was caught back in a high ponytail, and he could make out a suggestion of freckles dusting an upturned nose on a finely boned face. His eyes roamed her face. She didn't appear to be wearing any makeup, not even lipstick on provocatively full lips. Then he met her gaze. Amber eyes, and they were staring at him.

For a second, she looked as though she knew him, and for some reason, that didn't please her. Her eyes narrowed, and her mouth tightened, losing all the softness in her lips. She held his gaze almost defiantly and for what seemed forever, and he knew for a fact he'd never met her before. He had a gift for remembering people. It was in his best interests as a casino and hotel owner, to remember guests and clients. She'd never been either, and he'd never looked into those amber eyes before. He would have remembered. Any man would have remembered her.

The door started to slide shut and she reached out one slender hand to stop it. She exhaled harshly, then moved toward him, never taking her eyes off his. Before he could step out of the way, she veered to her right, ducked her head and was leaving. She headed for the door he'd just come through, and he was shocked that she could cover so much area so quickly without running.

This time, he reached for the elevator door before it could close and grabbed at the edge, but he didn't glance away. She was at the side door as she pulled a bright yellow knit hat out of her pocket and tugged it on over her brilliant hair. That was when she glanced back at him, giving away no surprise that he was watching her. Then she opened the door and was gone.

He stared at the closed door, feeling oddly off balance from the encounter. He didn't know why.

He got into the elevator. The door slid shut behind him, and he hit the Up button. He glanced at his reflection in the elevator door, halfway expecting to see that he had transformed into Mr. Hyde, or maybe grown a second head. No horns, no fangs, no warts. He'd had people not like him before, and he hadn't cared. Maybe she was one of Jack's friends, and they'd fought. Maybe she hated all men right now. He'd have to ask Jack what was going on.

The elevator stopped, the door slid back and Cain stepped into Jack's office area. It fronted Jack's private suite at the back of the turret he occupied. The plush leather, mahogany and leaded-glass windows were as mellow as Cain remembered. But the space was absolutely empty. There were no papers on the desk near the bank of windows that overlooked the slopes far below. There were no open books on the table by the chairs turned to face the massive stone fireplace. There was no fire in the hearth, and no sounds at all.

"Jack!" he called as he strode toward the partly closed door across the room. "Hey, Jack!"

He touched the door and it swung back. Jack was nowhere in sight. The expansive room, with a fireplace that matched the one in the office, was as empty as the rest of the place. Cain went to the right, into the kitchen, which was all stainless steel and ceramic tile, but there wasn't even the ever-present coffee brewing in the coffeemaker. Back out in the main area, he crossed to the double doors that led into Jack's bedroom. If Jack was in the bedroom, that meant that the woman had come from—

A noise in Jack's office cut short his thoughts. Quick footsteps sounded, then Jack came through the door. He stopped and stared at Cain as if he didn't recognize him for a moment, then his face broke into a huge smile. "Well, I'll be," he said as he walked to where Cain stood, his hands outstretched. "I didn't believe you'd come."

He grabbed Cain's shoulders, and although there was no hug or anything that bordered on mush, Cain was touched by Jack's greeting. "Good to see you, too," he muttered. As Jack drew back, Cain awkwardly slapped Jack on his shoulder. "I pay off my bets."

Jack eyed him up and down, then shrugged. "When you didn't show up earlier, I had my doubts." It was then that Cain realized Jack was in outer clothes—a denim, fur-lined jacket, with jeans and heavy boots darkened by clinging snow. "Sit, and let me get you a drink, then you can go over to number twenty." Jack talked as he headed back across the room. He took off the denim jacket and tossed it on the nearest chair, then walked his way out of his boots as he crossed to a bar built into the wall by the bedroom door. "What do you want to drink?" he asked.

"Anything," Cain murmured.

As a liquor bottle clinked against glasses, he spoke without looking back at Cain, "Did you get my message about Joshua?"

Cain had picked up the message moments before he'd left Las Vegas. Joshua Pierce, former cop in Atlanta and a widower for eighteen months, had suddenly found someone who had won him over so completely and quickly that he was getting married again two days before Christmas, right here at the Inn. "Yeah, I got it."

"And?" Jack queried as he turned with two glasses in his hands.

"And what?" Cain asked while he shrugged out of his leather jacket and tossed it on the couch nearest him before sinking into the supple leather cushions.

Jack came to him, held out one of the drinks, and Cain took it, cradling it in his hands as Jack sat on the couch opposite him. "So, what do you think?" Jack spoke as he settled. "One of the Great Four bites the dust."

Cain smiled at the title they'd given themselves so many years ago. Joshua, Jack, Cain and Gordie. "Yeah, the Great Four," he murmured, and sipped the amber liquid. Brandy—good, smooth brandy—and it hit the spot. "But Joshua did it before with Sarah." Cain shrugged. He'd only met his friend's wife once, yet he'd known right away why Joshua had fallen in love with her. But that didn't mean he understood why Joshua'd had chosen marriage then, or why he was choosing it again.

Jack lifted his glass, drank a bit, then sat back, crossing one leg over the other, his stockinged foot resting on his knee. "I didn't think he'd ever get married again, but you never know." He settled his glass on his thigh. "I'm aware of your aversion to weddings. You'll be here for it, won't you?"

He'd return for it. He'd decided that he would. "Sure, I'll be here."

Jack appeared pleased. "Good, so you'll be here through Christmas. Great, great," he murmured.

"No." Cain shook his head, cutting off that assumption as quickly as he could. "I'll come back for it. I can't stay."

Jack sat forward abruptly. "The deal was—"

"I'd come here around the holidays, and I have. I'm here and I'll spend a couple of days around town, then I have to get back. This is the busiest time of the year for the Dream Catcher and—"

"Oh, stop," Jack said with a frown. "Spare me. I remember the drill. You're busy. You're irreplaceable. You're indispensable. You made the damn place, and it can't stay standing without you there to support it."

"That about sums it up," Cain said with a smile, trying to lighten the tension starting in his neck and shoulders.

Jack wasn't smiling. "I'm not joking."

Cain shrugged and finished off the last of his drink. "Then my question is, why aren't you joking? What's so important that you need me here?"

He expected Jack to get angry again, or to pass the question off. He never expected him to say, "I'm not sure."

He twirled his empty glass. "Why not?"

Jack shrugged and exhaled on a heavy sigh. "At first I just thought we'd have a good time, relive our glory days." He did smile then, but fleetingly. "But lately I've been thinking that I need to change my life."

That was when Cain remembered the woman he'd faced in the elevator. The woman with fiery hair and amber eyes. "Who is she?"

Jack seemed genuinely perplexed by the question. "What?"

"The woman?"

"What woman?"

Cain sat forward and put his glass on the huge leather ottoman between the couches. He met Jack's gaze. "Does red hair, gold eyes and a look that could stop you in your tracks mean anything to you?" Jack was either a good actor or honestly confused. "Tiny? Madder than a wet hen? What did you do—break up with her, tell her to get out and she took off?"

Jack sat forward, suddenly intent. "When did you see her?"

"When I was coming up, she was leaving."

Jack glanced at his watch, then muttered, "Oh, damn, I thought I told her four."

"A missed date?"

"A missed appointment," Jack said, tossing back the last of his brandy. "She was here on business and I wasn't."

Cain didn't ask what "business." "Does she have anything to do with you wanting to change your life?"

"Not directly," Jack said as he got up and carried both empty glasses to the bar. He came back, handed Cain a new drink, then sat to face him again. "To the future…to whatever it holds," he said as he raised his own glass.

Cain answered his salute. "Yes, to whatever it holds."

HOLLY MARIE WINSTON felt flushed, and even though it was freezing outside, she turned the heater in her small blue car to its lowest setting. She drove out through the entry gates of the Inn at Silver Creek and went north, heading away from the Inn's almost oppressive luxury.

She'd all but decided not to meet with Jack Prescott, but had known she had to. She'd called up to Jack Prescott's suite from the front desk, and a man named Malone had met her at the private elevator. He'd let her in, said that Mr. Prescott would be right with her, then left through the private side entrance.

She'd waited for half an hour, horribly uncomfortable in the suite that had been empty when she'd arrived. She'd stood amid Jack Prescott's luxury, and gazed out the windows toward the ski runs and beyond to the mountain. *Her* mountain. That wouldn't change. She'd known that she shouldn't have come. She wasn't even going to stay to tell Prescott the mountain wasn't for sale. She'd left and that was when she'd come face-to-face with Cain Stone.

Her heart was still beating faster than it should from the brief encounter with the man, from the moment her eyes had met his. Cain Stone. Light snow started to fall, and she flipped on her windshield wipers, then her headlights to cut into the gray failing light of late afternoon.

She'd felt relieved that Jack hadn't kept their appointment, and she'd felt a sense of freedom, resolving to call him later and tell him her land wasn't for sale. The euphoria had lasted until the elevator door had opened and Cain Stone had stood in front of her.

She'd never seen him in person, only in pictures, but she hadn't been prepared for the height of the man—a few inches over six feet—or the width of the shoulders covered by an obviously expensive leather jacket. Long legs were encased in dark slacks, and he'd had a presence that had almost stopped her breathing when she'd first met his blue eyes.

Burning anger had surged through her. And it had grown when she saw him studying her, almost smiling, as if he were going to exchange pleasantries with her. The anger had overwhelmed her; all she'd thought about was getting out of there as quickly as she could, to get to anyplace she could breathe. She grimaced when she thought about how she'd almost run from him and about her last look back at him.

She flexed her hands on the steering wheel when she realized she was holding it in a death grip. She slowed as she passed the last of the property that Jack Prescott owned and kept going north. After a few minutes, she took a left turn onto a narrow road that climbed high up the mountain.

Cain Stone had obviously been going to see Jack Prescott, and that made sense. They'd been friends for years. Or maybe they were two big wheelers and dealers doing business. That was the only reason she'd been there. Business.

She slowed even more as the climb increased and stared straight ahead, thankful that the road had been cleared enough for her to use it. Then she saw her turnoff, went left again, onto a narrow road that had been plowed only on one side, so that just a single car at a time could use it. The snow was piled high on the right, where the mountain soared into the sky. There was little to no bank of cleared snow on her left, because the land dropped away, out of sight.

She went as far as the snowplow had cleared, then stopped, shut off the motor and got out. The air was bitingly cold up here, and a wind had come up, sweeping in a strange moaning sound across the deep snow, through the blanketed pines and into the gorge. She pulled her hat lower and pushed her hands into her pockets. She hadn't been up here since she'd gotten back in town. She hadn't thought about the place until Jack had contacted her. Now she wanted to see it again.

She walked into the untouched snow that covered the road-way, thankful she had on her calf-high boots. As the ridges swept back farther from the road she spotted what she was look-ing for. The snow all but obscured the driveway to the cabin, but a huge single pine at the road marked it for her. The same tree, feet taller now, but still there under the heavy weight of snow.

She climbed the steep grade, and she knew she wouldn't see the cabin until she hit the rise in the drive. Moments later it was there, the old cabin, appearing incredibly small, dwarfed by the huge pines that canopied its steeply pitched roof. She made her way to the wraparound porch, the only place with any protection from the snow.

She felt her foot hit the wood stairs, then she went up onto the porch and over to the door. She turned back to glance at the way she'd just walked, seeing her footsteps in the virgin snow. She was probably the first person to be here since her father had died. Her mother had been dead for ten years, and Annie, her half sister, wouldn't have any reason to trek up here. The place was Holly's, and now she was here. But as she looked around, she didn't want to be here alone.

Memories of her as a child driving up here for her weekly visits with her father rushed at her. She shivered, but it wasn't from the cold. *Not today,* she suddenly decided. She'd return when she was prepared to go inside and walk back into the part of the world she'd left behind her when she'd gone away from Silver Creek.

For a moment, in the frigid silence all around her, she felt an isolation that was almost painful. Maybe she'd thought that coming to the mountain would bring back that slim connection she'd had with her father. But there was nothing like that today. She exhaled, her breath curling into the cold air, then she walked away, stepping in her own footprints as she headed back to her car.

Her cell phone rang in her pocket just as she got to the end of the snowed-in driveway, startling her. She had no idea there was service up here. Even in town, the reception could be spotty at best. She took her cell phone out, flipped it open and saw a number that she recognized. She hit Send and said, "Mr. Prescott?"

"'Jack,' please, and I'm sorry I missed you. Can we reschedule?"

She kept walking. "There's no reason to." She was at her car now, and breathing hard from her efforts, or maybe from the tension starting to creep into her neck. Probably a mixture of both. "I'm not selling."

"You said we could talk."

"I thought about it, but I was at the Inn to tell you that I'm keeping the cabin and the land."

She got in the car, started the motor, closed the door as he spoke in her ear. "Don't make this—" his words began to break up "—discuss this and we—" Another break.

"It's a bad connection," she said, flipping the heater onto High.

"Mrs. Winston?" he said, louder now. "Are you—"

"I'll call you later," she said and didn't wait to hear if he answered or not. She shut the phone and tossed it on the seat beside her. "But the answer is still no," she said to the emptiness around her.

She turned in her seat to back down the road, and when she got to the main road, she headed south to Silver Creek. Her phone rang again. She checked the LED readout, saw it was Jack Prescott and let the call go to her message box. A moment later she got the beep that said she had a new voice mail. She ignored that, too.

She passed the entrance to the resort, glanced at the gates that were open to let a huge, silver SUV out. Cain Stone was behind the wheel, she noted. She hit the gas, heard her tires squeal slightly, and knew he'd probably glanced up at the sound. But she didn't wait to find out. She headed for town, looking neither right nor left at the skiing community, or at the Christmas decorations stretched high over the street lined with old brick and stone buildings.

By the time she'd pulled into the side parking area of the three-story Silver Creek Hotel, she was shaking. She sat in the car and stared at the building, the original hotel in Silver Creek, built during the silver strikes in the mid-1800s. Annie and her husband had bought it a few years earlier and restored it, saving it from becoming a boutique or a specialty coffee shop. Holly took several deep breaths, then made herself get out of her car and go inside.

She went into the warm air of the lobby, into a world of the past, with rich woods and brass everywhere. The old-fashioned check-in desk, with an antique pigeonhole letter sorter hung behind it, filled the far wall. The fragrance of gingerbread touched the air, and Christmas carols played softly in the background. "Annie?" she called at the same moment her half sister came through a curtained opening behind the desk.

Annie had Sierra in her arms, and once the two-year-old saw her mother, she wiggled out of Annie's arms and darted across the polished plank floors right for Holly. "Mommy!" she squealed as she threw herself into her mother's arms.

Holly swept her daughter up and hugged her, not realizing how tightly she was holding onto Sierra until the little girl squirmed and pushed back. Her daughter had the same hair as hers, a coppery red, done in braids that Annie had taken time fashioning. Her chubby face was sprinkled with freckles and her eyes were as blue as the overalls she was wearing. Holly found herself hoping that eye color was all Sierra had gotten from her father.

Holly let Sierra down, watched her run back behind the desk, then go into the room beyond the curtain. Annie stayed behind the desk. "Don't worry," she said, "Uncle Rick's in there to watch her." Then she asked, "So, was Jack mad, or did he up the offer?"

Holly moved closer to Annie. Her half sister was taller than her, with nondescript brown hair, gray eyes and a face wreathed in smiles. Holly was always amazed at how upbeat Annie was almost all the time. Maybe it was the fact they had two different fathers. Annie's father, Norman Day, had died when Annie was four, so she barely remembered him. But the people around town still said what a wonderful man he'd been.

A year after Norman's death, their mother had married Scott Jennings, Holly's dad. The people around town hadn't liked him then, and still didn't speak well of him. She'd never figured out why her mother had married him, or why they'd only been married long enough for her to be born before her dad had gone to live at his cabin and her mother had stayed in town to work at the diner. "He never showed for the meeting."

Annie heard laughter from Sierra behind the curtains and called without looking back, "Rick, make sure she doesn't kill the gingerbread men."

"One down, eleven to go," her husband called back.

Annie laughed but didn't take her eyes off Holly. "If he didn't show, then you have more time to think this through and make sure you know what you're doing."

Holly skimmed her yellow knit hat off and pushed it in her pocket, then undid her jacket. "I'm not selling," she said.

"Why not?" Annie asked. "Just tell me why you're not going to take all that money and laugh all the way to the bank?"

Holly shrugged. "The cabin's mine," she said. "It's…" She bit off the rest of her words—*It's all I have left of Dad.* Annie wouldn't understand that at all. She was one of the people who had hated Scott Jennings. "It's what I have for Sierra, for her future. It's really all I have."

Annie exhaled. "I know, but if you think about it—"

"Annie, no, I've made up my mind."

"Okay, okay, fine." She held up her hands in a gesture of surrender. "It's yours. You can do what you want with it, and I understand it's all that your dad left you. Mom didn't have anything." Annie's smile was fading now, and Holly never doubted that Annie blamed Scott Jennings for a lot. Then she flicked her eyes over Holly. "I'm sorry, I didn't mean to upset you."

Holly shook her head. "You didn't. It's not you," she admitted.

Annie watched Holly. "Then what's wrong?"

"Who."

"Oh, not Travis again," she said, with absolutely no smile now. "That crummy son-of-a—"

"It's nothing to do with Travis." Her ex-husband had actually left her alone since she'd returned to Silver Creek. "He's doing his thing somewhere, and he doesn't have time to worry about me or Sierra."

"Then what is it?"

"Cain Stone. I just saw him."

Annie's eyes widened and her lips formed a perfect circle of surprise. "Where?"

"At the Inn." Memory flashed of the moment she'd spotted him, that second when she'd realized who he was and when she'd felt all the anger she'd had for so long, about so many things. "I think he was going up to see Jack Prescott."

Annie eyed her. "What did you say to him?"

"Nothing. I left." She ran. "What good would it do to say anything to him? He wouldn't care. They don't call him 'Stone Cold' for nothing."

Annie shrugged. "We never called him that, but I'm sure we called him 'Raising Cain' more than once."

Holly reflected on the blue eyes—hard, cold blue eyes—of the man she'd seen today. A man who, she'd bet, never lost any sleep over the chaos he left in his wake. "I'm sure that fits, too," she murmured.

Chapter Two

When Cain stepped into one of the most exclusive cabins at the Inn, one that was usually kept available for some of Jack's high-profile celebrities who used the Inn to "disappear" from their hectic lives for a while, he was already wondering when he could go back to Las Vegas. The multilevel cabin, nestled in the rugged land near the ski slopes, had more than a thousand square feet but only three rooms. The bedroom took up the whole top level, with views of the ski runs and, in the distance, the resort and the town. The living area was a rambling space, with two fireplaces, three levels and supple leather everywhere. The kitchen took up almost a third of the lower level.

But he barely glanced at it. Instead, he found the phone nearest the entrance, made a few quick calls to check on business, then crossed to the windows and looked out at the late afternoon. If he had to stay, skiing seemed particularly inviting. Yet it was too late. The light was still okay, but here when the sun went down, skiing it was over for the day. He didn't want to use the main slope, which had lights on twenty-four hours a day. No, he wanted the slope he remembered as a kid, to get the rush he remembered when he'd skied the Killer years ago.

He headed for the door. He had no idea where Jack was, so he got in his SUV and headed for the gates. Once he'd driven off the grounds of the resort, he headed south to Silver Creek. The Inn was two miles north of the main part of town, with a buffer of empty land in between.

He drove away from the world of the rich and famous to the world of Silver Creek, the town he'd grown up in. He'd never been given to nostalgia, always reasoning that you had to have good memories to indulge in that sort of thing. But at the moment, he felt an odd sense of longing to see the town again. Not the main street, but the back parts, the parts he remembered from his childhood.

He drove along the snow-lined streets at a snail's pace. The town was overrun with the influx of skiers and with businesses catering to their needs. There were upscale restaurants, convenience stores, boutiques and supply stores that held every sort of ski product you could imagine. When he'd been here years ago, skiing had been a sport you did, usually on raw runs that you cut yourself. Now skiers lined up at the lifts, bought tickets and skied where they were told to ski.

In the old-town section, he glanced at the buildings that had been refurbished and repurposed into boutiques, ski supply places, coffee shops and souvenir corners. A few held to their origins, like Rusty's Diner on the east side of the street, a plain place with good food and still managed by Rusty himself. Rollie's Garage, the same garage that Rollie Senior had operated years ago was still there, now run by his son. On a side street he saw the original police station, where Joshua's father had been sheriff all those years ago.

Although he now knew where he was going, he hadn't realized it until that moment he saw Eureka Street. He slowed to a crawl when he approached the only building to the right. The old, two-story brick structure appeared the same, pretty much how it had when he'd been a sixteen-year-old sneaking out at dawn on a day as cold and snowy as this one.

He felt drawn back into the past, and despite the painfully new sign above the double-door entry, Silver Creek Medical Clinic, he could have been a kid again. Back then the sign over the doors had read Silver Creek Children's Shelter—a euphemism for *orphanage.* He pulled onto the half-circle drive that ran past the entry. Snow was piled high on either side, but a section had been cleared to make it easy for anyone to get to the doors.

He stared at the building for a long moment, at the lights spilling out the bottom windows onto the snow and the deep shadows on either side. The place looked old and dark, the way it always had, and he barely controlled a sudden shudder. He'd thought he'd go in and find Gordie, but now he decided against it. He'd didn't want to step onto the green tiled floors or hear the empty echo that seemed to always be in the old building. He'd see Gordie at the Inn.

He meant to drive out to the street, then go back to the Inn, but he found himself stopping at the end of the drive and looking at the school directly across the street from the clinic. His gaze skimmed the old brick building, the Christmas decorations in the tall, narrow windows of the bottom floor and two huge wreaths on the double front doors at the top of recently cleared concrete steps. The only change was the fairly new six-foot-high chain-link fence that enclosed the whole area, including the parking lot. The lot's double gates were open, and a snowplow sat idly nearby. A fraction of the lot had been cleared before whoever drove the plow had stopped for the day.

Cain went straight across the street, through the open gates and onto the asphalt parking area. He passed the still plow and slipped into one of the few cleared parking slots, one of five or six fronted by blue signs designating the user. He felt a hint of a smile when he chose the one marked "Reserved for the Principal" instead of the one marked "Reserved for the Librarian."

Over the school's main doors a banner rippled in the wind, proclaiming CHRISTMAS FESTIVAL, DEC. 24, 7:00 P.M. They'd had Christmas programs when he'd been there, but he'd never had anyone to come and see him. After the concert he got the candy canes the town Santa handed out. Everyone had known the Santa was Charlie Sloan's dad, a cop at the police station. But they'd all pretended to be excited and believe he was *the* Santa.

Cain hadn't bothered with the make-believe. He'd taken what he could, then gone back to the orphanage, to wake up on Christmas morning to a neatly wrapped present that had always held clothes some well-meaning town person had donated to the orphanage. He hadn't expected much else. It had simply been his life. Just as his life now was his life. But now it was all up to him to get what he wanted, instead of waiting for some Good Samaritan to give the "poor orphan" something he needed.

He hadn't had the desire to go into the clinic moments earlier, but now he found himself getting out of his car to go into the school. Snow was starting to fall softly from the gray heavens, and it brushed his face. He shoved his hands into the pockets of his leather jacket as he went toward the entry and took the steps in a single stride.

He pushed against the heavy wood-and-glass doors, but the door was locked tight. He cupped his hands on the cold glass and leaned to peer inside. Security lights showed the expansive center hallway. Lockers lined both sides of the walls, and the same highly polished tiles were still on the floor. Christmas was everywhere, from the paper garlands looping high on the walls to the Christmas tree, done in red, green, silver and gold, just inside the door.

He could almost see the kids in the hallway, the bustle of life, back then. He could remember the smell of new books and new pencils, the shouts of friends heard above the daily announcements blaring over the loudspeakers. Then that was gone, and all he felt was an emptiness that was almost tangible to him. He pulled back from the door, ready to leave. But as he turned to go, he saw a small blue car turn into the parking area, disappear behind the large plow for a moment, then come back into view as it pulled into the slot he'd forgone, the one for the librarian.

The windows in the car were partially fogged up, but he could make out a single occupant. The motor stopped, the door opened and he found himself looking at the woman from the elevator. She stepped out into the cold, and glanced up at him, her forehead tugged into a frown under her bright yellow knit cap.

"You," she said, her breath curling into the cold air, the single word sounding like an accusation.

He wasn't an egotist, but most women didn't study him as if he were an insect. At that moment, this woman was regarding him with the same contempt she'd shown earlier. At least, he thought that was the expression on her face as she hurried over to the stairs and came up quickly to stand one step below him. She was just as tiny as he remembered. Now, standing on the step above her as he was, he towered over her by at least a foot.

She tilted her face up, and he saw tendrils of her brilliant hair that had escaped her yellow knit cap clinging to her temple and her cheek. Her amber eyes were narrowed on him as if she didn't like what she saw, and her voice was brusque when she asked, "What are you doing here?"

He found himself forcing a smile, but there was no humor in him at all. "I'm going to blow the place up," he said with heavy sarcasm. "How about you?"

Red suddenly dotted her cheeks and her expression tightened even more. She exhaled in a rush. "You don't belong here."

He wouldn't argue with that. He never had belonged here. Not here, not anywhere. "I went to this school back in the Stone Age, and I was just looking around."

"For old times' sake?" she muttered.

He shrugged. That was as good an explanation as any he could come up with at the moment. "Sure, old times' sake." He hadn't meant to be sarcastic then, but he was. He glanced down, and saw a ring of keys in her gloved hand. "What are you doing here with keys?"

"I work here. I teach second grade, or I will be teaching second grade when school's back in session after the holidays."

A teacher? He never had a teacher like her when he was here. "Well, I won't keep you," he murmured, and went down the stairs.

He couldn't tell if he heard her say "Goodbye" as he walked away, but he heard the door open, then close, followed by the sound of a lock being set. As he got in his car and settled behind the wheel, he realized he didn't even know her name. He'd never asked. He glanced back at the school and was taken aback to see the woman with no name looking out the glass top of the door at him. And the woman with no name wasn't smiling.

Cain read people well. He could size up someone at ten feet and be pretty close to being right about the person. Maybe owning a casino had something to do with having that particular skill, or maybe it was a skill he'd honed throughout his life. Strangers had come and strangers had gone, and it had always been up to him to figure out why anyone was near him, and what they wanted from him.

But this woman baffled him, this woman didn't fit into any of the categories he used when he labeled people. She was pretty enough, in a small, delicate way. A teacher. And she hated him.

He drove out of the parking lot, even though he had the most overwhelming need to go back and confront her. He just wanted to understand. But he didn't turn back. He drove north, and by the time he got to the Inn and his cabin, he realized he'd never confront her. He'd never see her again. He'd leave, and she'd be teaching her hellions at the start of the new year. He shrugged as he went in a side door to his cabin, into comfortable heat. What she thought of him just didn't matter.

As HOLLY SAT BACK in her chair behind her desk, which was heavy with paperwork, the silence of the empty classroom weighed heavily on her. She wasn't able to concentrate, not with her thoughts on the one person she didn't even want to think about—Cain Stone. First the shock of seeing the man in person, then Annie's reaction to her reaction to Cain Stone.

"That's just plain irrational," Annie had said while Sierra destroyed more gingerbread men. "You've never even talked to him."

She had talked to him. Once. When she was seven or maybe eight. He'd been up on the mountain, ready to ski the hard run without permission. It was their land, not some teen-agers', who had seemed to her to take great delight in taunting her father. Her father had yelled at them, and she could remember she'd yelled, too.

The boys, four of them altogether, had waited until she and her father had gotten close; then, one by one, they had taken off down the run. They'd skied out of sight and never looked back. She still remembered their laughter echoing in the cold air. Then one year they didn't come to ski. She didn't think they ever were there again.

"He ran away," Annie had said to her. "He took off when he was sixteen and no one knew for years where he went. Then he showed up in Las Vegas, and the rest, as they say, is history."

Her history, she thought bitterly. She'd heard the name Cain Stone a year ago, and it had changed her whole life. She gave up working at her desk, got up, gathered her things and left the school. She didn't have far to drive to get to the house she'd rented for herself and Sierra. But by the time she was inside, she was freezing.

Quickly, she lit the fire she'd laid in the fireplace of the old bungalow, then went into her room. The place had been rented furnished, with nondescript pieces. A brown couch, two matching chairs, knotty pine end tables and a braided rug in the living room. Her bedroom had a double-sized, metal bedstead, with a single dresser and another braided rug. Sierra's room had a single bed, a chest of drawers and about the only thing, besides their clothes, she'd brought with them from Las Vegas—her crib.

Without looking around, Holly stripped, stepped into a hot shower and stood there for a very long time. When she finally got out, the room was fogged with steam. She could hear the phone in the bedroom ringing. She grabbed her robe to put around her, then hurried into the bedroom and picked up the phone by her bed. "Hello?" she said a bit breathlessly.

"Holly, it's Jack Prescott."

She sank onto the bed and closed her eyes. After the failed meeting, and the aborted phone call, she'd decided that she'd write him a letter, refusing his offer, and leave it at that. "Yes?"

"Sorry to miss the meeting. I got my times mixed up. And phone service up here is pretty awful. I called you earlier to find out when it would be convenient to meet again."

"I don't think we need to."

"You can come here or we can meet wherever you want to," he said as if she hadn't spoken at all.

"There's no reason to meet. The land isn't for sale."

He was silent for a moment, then named a figure that made her blink. "How about that?" he asked.

"I really don't—"

He cut her off. "Think about it, and I'll call you tomorrow. We can talk then," he said, and disconnected.

She'd barely hung up, when the phone rang again. She picked up the receiver. "Hello?"

"Hey, babe."

The voice of her ex-husband on the other end made her cringe. "What do you want, Travis?"

"Is that any way to answer the phone?"

Travis never called unless he wanted something, and she just didn't have any more to give him, in any sense of the word. "What do you want?" she repeated.

"I called to find out how you and the kid are doing. Can't I do that?"

He could, but he hadn't. "You're going to see Sierra on Christmas, aren't you?"

Travis spoke quickly. "Yeah, sure, of course." But she knew he wasn't, and she'd have to explain to her daughter why her daddy wasn't there. "The thing is, I'm strapped. I want to get the kid something really nice, and if you could send me some money, maybe three hundred, just a loan?"

She fought the urge to slam the phone down. Instead, she bit her lip, then said, "I don't have it."

"Oh, come on. Borrow it from your sister or something. She's got that hotel, and she's not hurting for money."

"Travis, I'm not asking Annie for money for you."

"Hell, she's crazy about the kid. Tell her it's for the Christmas present."

She wouldn't lie like that, not when the money would go into the nearest blackjack or poker game. "No, I won't," she said, hating the slight unsteadiness in her voice. "The locket was the last thing you'll get from me."

She hadn't meant to say that. The locket was long gone, but losing it had been the last straw, what had prompted her to walk out. Travis uttered a harsh expletive and hung up. She fell back on the bed and stared at the ceiling.

She'd left Las Vegas because of Travis and the life they'd had there. She'd returned to Silver Creek, a place that had always been a cocoon of safety for her. But nothing had changed. Not with Travis. He'd violated her peace and so had Cain Stone.

"Damn them both," she muttered as she turned onto her side. She balled her hand into a fist and hit the pillow over and over. Tears burned her eyes, and she fought them. She wasn't going to cry. She was going to make a life for herself in Silver Creek, despite Travis, despite Cain Stone.

CAIN HAD ALWAYS BEEN a night person, going to bed near dawn most days. But that night at the Inn, he got into bed around midnight and slept until dawn crept into the room. He woke up instantly, sleep completely gone. He'd had the strangest dreams, snippets of ideas, all jumbled, about teachers and detention and forgotten lessons and brilliant hair around a beautiful face that—in the dreams, at least—had smiled at him.

When his body seemed to have ideas that were ridiculous, Cain rolled out of bed and headed for the elaborate bathroom. No, cave. The walls, floor and ceiling were fashioned from rock and stone, with a sunken Jacuzzi in the middle of the floor, positioned perfectly for the view out stone-arched windows that overlooked the main ski runs. He passed it by in favor of the open shower, a three-sided structure built into the rock of the mountainside. A waterfall ran out the back wall, and with a flick of a switch, the waterfall became rain falling from overhead in varying strengths, from a mere sprinkle to a deluge. Side jets massaged the body at the same time.

He flicked the switch and warm water rained down on him immediately. He tipped his head back, letting the water run over his face. Despite the soothing water, he felt edgy and tense. And the dream's images refused to evaporate under the steamy spray. Finally, he got out and reached for a towel. As he started to dry himself, he glanced out the windows to the high slopes in the distance and remembered what he'd decided the evening before. There it was. The mountain. Killer Run.

Dawn was bathing the mountain in its glow, and he suddenly felt like a kid who was going to play hooky. This was probably because of all those crazy dreams about the teacher. He decided to do something he'd done a lot when he was a kid—take off with his skis on his shoulder, heading for the mountain.

He tossed the towel on a side shelf and reached for a house phone, set into a rock niche next to the trio of sinks under more windows. He hit the star button, and even though a glance at the nearest clock said it was only five-twenty in the morning, the call was answered on the second ring.

"Good morning, sir. This is Alfred. How may I be of assistance to you?"

"I want to go skiing," he said.

Before he could add anything, Alfred said, "Very good. Have your requirements on file changed?"

Cain didn't know he had any requirements on file. "What do you have?"

Alfred read off a list without hesitation, from Cain's shirt size to his preference in ski bindings. Everything sounded right, even the fact that he liked down vests and not jackets, that he liked thermals under his clothes, that he favored bands instead of hats and liked reds. Jack had fed Alfred all the information and he'd noted everything.

"Nothing's changed," Cain said.

"When will you be needing your supplies?" Alfred asked.

"Within half an hour?"

"Absolutely," Alfred replied without a second's hesitation. "Is there anything else, sir?"

"Coffee."

"Espresso? Cappuccino? Café mocha? Latte? Cinam—"

"Just coffee," he said, cutting off the recitation. "Just black, please."

"Colombian? Afric—"

"Anything. Just make sure it's hot," he said.

"Yes, sir," Alfred said.

Good to his word, Alfred had the supplies at Cain's cabin in twenty minutes, along with strong black coffee in a thermal carafe. He drank most of the coffee before he put on the thermals, then black ski pants and a white turtleneck pullover over them. He shrugged into the red down vest and tried the boots. They were a perfect fit. Damn, Jack was good, Cain thought with real admiration. He slipped on reflective glasses, drained the last of his coffee, then grabbed his bundled skis and poles and left.

When he was a kid, he'd walked all the way from the orphanage, but had cut across Jack's land, which had been untouched back then. He'd climb every inch of the way to the ridge—no lifts or rides of any kind then, either. He'd leave about three in the morning to get there by sunrise, and sometimes Jack and Joshua, maybe even Gordie, would be there waiting for him. Then they took the run together.

The Inn operated its lifts 24/7 even if no one used them. Convenience was everything at the Inn, and Cain took the easy way up. He rode on the lower lift, caught a ride at the halfway point on another lift, then switched to the one that went closest to Killer Run.

He got off at the top but kept going upward, managed to climb over the confinement fence that marked the edge of the Inn's property, and headed for the trees that lined the east side of the run. He traveled parallel to them as he trudged higher, studying the sweep of the run as he went, watching for any hazards hidden under the snow. Downed trees, rocks, anything could be concealed under the whiteness, but you got to where you could read the snow itself, the shape, the way it flowed, any intrusions in the way it hugged the mountain.

His breath curled around his face as he struggled to make the top. As a kid, he'd made the top easily. Now it was work, not like taking elevators up and down at the hotel or working out on a treadmill. But worth it, he knew when he saw Killer Run.

It was beyond a series of ridges that jutted out into the air from the mountainside. If you hit the top of the run just right, you'd clear the ridges. If you didn't, the ground below was deep with snow and hopefully you'd land safely, missing rocks and small trees. He'd always been lucky that way.

Now he climbed, ignoring old signs that said Private Property and No Skiing—Danger! Jack had mentioned that Old Man Jennings had died and he was working with his heir. So there wouldn't be a frantic man screaming at Cain and ordering him off the mountain.

The sun was up completely, the day keenly bright with light glinting off the fresh snow, and his glasses tinted everything slightly blue. His boots sank calf-deep in the snow, and he climbed much more slowly as he went around the ridges and up the back way. He spotted the tree grouping he was looking for—a stand around a clearing at the top, right where the run started.

At last he stood on the top of the mountain, the heavens above him and the whole valley of Silver Creek below.

He took a deep breath of the thin, cold air, then jammed his skis and poles into the deep snow and just stared at the view. Beyond the grounds of the Inn, the town appeared like a Christmas-card scene, all white snow, the spread of quaint buildings, the distant ski lifts and the smoke from numerous chimneys drifting into the sky.

He studied the Inn. It was just as pleasant looking, but years and years newer from all the development. The scattering of expensive cottages, each positioned for the most privacy, gave the impression of being their own small town. Smoke curled into the air from many chimneys, and the main lodge spread out in both directions, nestling into the snowy land.

He lifted gloved hands, cupped them around his mouth and did something he'd done every time in the past. "Top of the world!" he yelled. The sound echoed clearly to him five times, then with the vaguest whisper of a sixth time, before it was gone.

"Six," he yelled, letting the single word come back to him over and over. "Still champ!" His voice was everywhere, then faded away. He reached for skis, put them down, stepped into the bindings and bent to fasten them. Then he stood, flexed his legs and made his way to the start of the run, the one spot that was perfectly aligned with the outcropping below.

He flexed his hands on the pole grips and was ready to push off, when he heard someone yell, "Hey, there!"

His lifted one ski, pivoted and looked behind him. He thought he glimpsed something yellow, then it was gone. It appeared again off to his right, and then the teacher broke out of the trees. She was skiing her way toward him. Her yellow knit hat was pulled low over her brilliant hair, the colors a vivid contrast with her dull gray jacket and ski pants. When she was four feet from him, she tilted her head back and peered up into his face.

The sight of her stirred something so basic in him that he had to inhale a deep breath to level out his thoughts. He took in the deep amber eyes, the lift of her chin, the flame of her hair. Old goggles hung around her neck, and plain knit gloves covered her hands. She wasn't his type—at least, he'd never thought "tiny and cute" could be sexy—but he knew better right then. He'd always been a risk taker in every sense of the word, and he had a niggling feeling that being attracted to this woman was risk taking at its best. He didn't back down. He didn't even care that she was staring at him as if he'd stolen the crown jewels.

Chapter Three

Holly spotted the red first, the flash of color where there shouldn't be color, then she'd heard the sound. The echoing voice that rang through the valley, bouncing off the mountains. She hesitated going closer, then couldn't stand not going to see who was there. Few ever got up this way, except... That made her move faster. Except Jack Prescott's people, surveying the land by hers. She dug in, partly gliding on the snow and partly sinking in spots. She awkwardly made her way to the sound. Through the trees she saw a single man by the ridge.

He yelled again, letting his voice echo at him, then he made a grab for his poles. Someone from the resort? One of Prescott's men? They were on her land. She hurried, shouted to him, "Hey, there!"

She went forward for the widest opening in the trees, pushing hard to move faster, and broke out of the snow-laden grove directly across from the single person. He was turning, the bloodred of his vest brilliant against the clear blue sky behind him. Fancy clothes, she thought, expensive skis. Reflective glasses that bounced back at her the glint of the morning sun. She skied closer to him, ready to tell him to get off her property, then she realized the intruder was Cain Stone.

That stopped her within two ski lengths of him. She took a gulping breath, then demanded, "What are you doing here?"

He looked unruffled at her arrival, almost as if he was enjoying it. "I'm not going to be basket weaving," he said with the hint of a smile twitching at his lips. She had no idea what was in his eyes. The glasses just reflected her own, distorted image.

She'd taken this run for years, and she had no doubt she could ski it, but she didn't know too many others who would even try, except Cain Stone and his cohorts years ago. Back then she'd thought they had to be either stupid or arrogant. Now she realized this man had to be both. "You aren't going to ski down, so why don't you go back that way." She motioned behind her. "There's a road about a quarter mile beyond the trees. If you're lucky, you can hitch a ride back to town."

She expected him to get angry or annoyed, but she didn't expect him to laugh right out loud. The sound echoed around them. "I don't hitchhike," he finally said.

"Do you read signs?"

"Every one of them."

"How about the Private Property signs you had to pass on the way here?"

His laughter was gone now. "I read every one of them."

"Then get off this land. It's private."

"I don't see a badge."

"What?"

"I assumed that you're some sort of security, policing this area."

She shook her head. "It's private land."

"Oh, and you own it?"

She stared right at him. "Damn straight I do."

She couldn't tell if she'd shocked him or not. His expression didn't change—at least, she didn't think it did. And she couldn't see his eyes. "How?" was all he said.

"How what?"

"How could you own it?"

"All you need to know is I own it. And this isn't a public run. It's posted, and—"

"The kid," he exclaimed. "You're the kid, aren't you?"

"What kid?"

"The hair. I remember the hair. Jennings coming after us, and you running up behind him, a tiny little thing, but with a booming voice." He smiled suddenly, an expression that shook her. "You'd yell, 'Get off my mountain,' while Jennings threatened to shoot us on the spot."

Her dad had been furious at their intrusion. "I'll skin them alive," he'd say. "Maybe shoot them, too." But he never caught up with them. As she and her father had come out of the trees, one by one the boys had turned and taken off. By the time she got to the edge, the boys were shooting down the run, their voices echoing into the mountains as they yelled, "Yahoo!" Then she'd go back to the cabin with her dad, and while she'd wait for her mother to pick her up, she'd keep the fire going and watch her father get drunker and drunker, all the while muttering about "those blasted teenagers."

"You were trespassing back then, too," she murmured, not wanting to remember that time of her life clearly.

"You're …" He thought for a second. "Molly?"

"It's Holly, and you're still trespassing."

He didn't move. "Tell me one thing, Holly."

"What?"

"Did he really have a gun?"

She was so shocked that she almost smiled. She didn't intend to smile with this man, or have this conversation. "No, he didn't, but he didn't want you on his land, and neither do I."

The next question rocked her. "Is that why you hate me? Because I used the run when Jennings didn't want me to?"

"What are you talking about?" she asked.

He actually came closer, his skis spreading right and left to go on the outside of hers. He got within two feet of her, and he towered over her. She forced herself not to retreat. If she moved, she'd fall into him, tangle with his skis, and this whole situation would be even more embarrassing.

He leaned toward her, erasing even more space between them. "You know, that look, as if I'm two rungs below the lowest rung on the ladder of humanity."

"You're crazy," she said quickly, but didn't sound very convincing even to her ears.

"Am I?" he asked, and she was certain she felt the suggestion of heat from his breath touch her face.

She shook her head. "Yes, you are."

"And you don't hate me?"

She couldn't tell a lie of that magnitude. "What difference would it make if I did?"

He was very still for a long moment. Then, without warning, he leaned even closer, cupped her chin with his gloved hand. "A hell of a lot of difference," he whispered roughly. Then he let her go before she could think of how to react, and expertly turned without hitting her skis. With a glance back at her, he moved to the edge of the run, dug in, and in the next instant he pushed off and was away. His voice echoed to her, "Yahoo!" over and over again.

She hurried to the edge, saw the path he cut in the snow and saw him take the jump at the outcropping with ease.

She'd been ready to ski the run herself, and she wasn't going to let him change her plans. She flipped up her goggles, then pushed off herself. Never glancing away from the bright red vest, she made the jump cleanly, and landed with knees bent at almost the exact spot he'd landed.

She kept going, her eyes on him ahead of her, and she saw his mistake an instant before he made it. She screamed, "Left, left," but there was no time for him to adjust. He didn't go left, kept going straight ahead, no doubt figuring that the even snow beyond was safe. But it wasn't. She knew it wasn't. There'd been a rock slide in the summer, and there was now a crater in the mountain where it hadn't been before. The snow that hid it was soft, and the instant he hit the softness, he sank. His skis caught, and he went flying forward, skis over head. She slowed, swept left and back, then she skied sideways to a stop near where he was sprawled awkwardly in the snow. One ski had been released from its bindings, coming to rest near his head, and the other ski was on its side, twisted with his foot. She couldn't see his poles anywhere.

She pushed with her poles, skied sideways, approaching the hole of snow, and carefully picked her way over to where he'd ended up, no more than three feet from a huge pine. He wasn't moving, just lying facedown in the snow. She didn't like him. She didn't like his kind, but that didn't stop her heart from rising in her throat. "Are you okay?" she yelled.

She bent down, unsnapped her bindings, then trudged over to him. She stooped by him, her knees sinking in the powdery snow. She reached for him, grabbing his vest, but was afraid to move him in case she did more harm to him than good. "Cain," she breathed. "Can you hear me?"

He stirred then, and she pulled back. He pushed one hand

into the snow, then slowly turned until he was on his back. His goggles were still in place and they reflected her image and caught the sunlight behind her. She couldn't see any blood on him, but he moved very cautiously as he lifted a hand to take off his glasses. She was looking into eyes filled with the same laughter that was twitching at his lips. "Face-plant," he muttered as he shoved himself up and realigned his single ski. "I haven't done that since…" He shrugged as he swiped at the snow that clung to his face and hair and grinned at her. "Too long ago to remember."

She sank back on her heels. "It's not funny. You could have killed yourself."

He swiped his glasses off, then slipped them back on. "I'm not dead. Just ended up with hurt pride," he murmured. "But it does hurt." He glanced past her up the hill. "What happened—rocks messed up or a sinkhole?"

"Rocks," she said. "They had a slide in the summer and it left a good-sized pocket."

"Well, live and learn," he said, pushing himself up to his feet. He turned to her and held out a gloved hand.

She ignored it and got to her feet herself. She brushed at her pants, then managed to make herself look up at him. She motioned to the east. "Go down that way and you're at the fence for the resort."

He reached for his errant ski and put it back on. Then he scanned the area. "My poles," he said, going past her. She watched him digging into the snow, then coming up with both poles. "Lucky they stuck together," he said.

"It doesn't bother you that you could have broken your neck?" She motioned to the huge pine that would have been his stopping place if the soft snow hadn't slowed him.

He came back to where she stood, meshing his skis with hers the way he had at the top. "Oh, I'm not worried about *my* neck," he said. "And what's life without taking chances." He grinned. "It's a rush."

"A face-plant is a rush?" she muttered.

He laughed. "I guess so."

"Just stay off my land," she said, and made her way to the run again. She paused, glanced over her shoulder and was taken aback to find him right behind her. "Go on to the fancy resort and use their runs."

"Sensible," he said. "But then again, I've never been accused of being sensible." He moved past her, shot her a quick look, then pushed off, heading farther down the run.

She watched him go, and knew she wasn't skiing anymore today. The time she'd wanted to spend alone, to sort out things, was gone. She undid her skis, put them and her poles over her shoulder and started back up. No lifts here, just good old-fashioned climbing. She heard a shout from below, but didn't turn. If he face-planted again, he was on his own.

That thought made her smile and she caught herself. It wasn't funny if he got hurt, yet she couldn't help but hope he was in the soft snow again, face first, and this time he wouldn't be able to find his poles.

CAIN MADE IT BACK to his cottage the long way around, skiing parallel to the resort until he got to the south end of the property and went in a service gate. By the time he'd walked to his cabin, he was ready for a hot shower and dry, clean clothes. But all the time he showered and cleaned up, his thoughts were on standing on the ridge at the top of the run.

The teacher who'd looked at him as though he were an insect was Holly, and Holly was the kid. The red-haired kid. The screamer. The little hellion who'd threatened him and his friends. He laughed as he soaped up in the shower. She'd grown up to be just as much a hellion. Teacher or not. She had a temper and she owned the land. Added to that, she was starting to bring out more than a bit of lust in him. He never thought he went for redheads or for tiny women. Certainly never a teacher. Everything Holly was. He laughed again softly as he stepped out of the shower.

He dried off and got dressed in black slacks, a black turtleneck and boots. He put on his leather jacket and went out again, choosing to walk to the main building. It was snowing lightly, and before he'd gone more than twenty feet, one of the electric carts used at the resort drove up to him. A bundled-up attendant was driving it.

"Sir? Where may I take you?"

Cain climbed in and said, "The lodge, to see Mr. Prescott."

"Yes, sir," the attendant said, and he took off quickly. He stopped at the side entrance, and smiled at Cain. "Dial star 9 and ask for James when you need a ride back."

"You bet, James," he said, then stepped out and headed to the door. Once inside, he went to the private elevator, punched in the code, and the doors opened. But this time the car was empty. No Holly. He hit the up button, and moments later he was stepping out of the elevator into Jack's outer room. He started for the inner door, but hesitated when he heard Jack speaking to someone.

"I've tried to understand this, but I can't. All I can come up with is you're going after more money, and if that's the case…" His words trailed off, and Cain waited by the door for someone to respond. When no one did, he assumed Jack was on the phone, and pushed the door back to step into Jack's suite.

He'd barely taken two steps, when he halted in his tracks. Jack wasn't on the phone at all. He was talking to Holly. She was sitting on one of the two sofas by the fireplace, and Jack was standing over her. His whole attitude was subtly intimidating, and in that moment, Cain didn't like it. He spoke up, getting their attention. "Well, look who's here," he drawled as he went closer to the two of them.

Both turned at the sound of his voice. Jack looked taken aback, but pleased. The man was in all black—another intimidation thing. Holly glanced at Cain, and he could see color dotting her cheeks; her mouth was set in a straight line. But this time the expression in her eyes wasn't for Cain. She was furious, and he realized it had to be with Jack. "You made it down?" he asked her.

She stood quickly, forcing Jack to back up or make contact. He chose to back up. She was on her feet, appearing very vulnerable, skin pale next to her flaming hair, and wearing old jeans and a loose sweatshirt with the UNLV logo on it. "I went up, but you made it, obviously," she said with a glance at him, before she looked back at Jack. "That's about all I have to say," she said, and moved away from Jack, toward Cain where she stopped and tilted her head to look up at him.

There was no anger in those amber eyes this time, just a subtle sense of—what? Desperation? Frustration? God, he wished he could read her expressions. She seemed so tiny in regular clothes, and he could see the rapid, shallow breaths lifting her high breasts under the old fleece of the sweatshirt. For the life of him, he couldn't figure out what this woman was thinking at any given time. She wasn't playing games; he was sure of that. There was no subtle baiting and flirting. Too bad, actually, that his lust, for lack of a better word, was so one-sided. "Can you move?" she asked in a low voice.

"I could," he murmured, and saw the color come back into her cheeks. Her eyes were getting brighter. Tears? That shocked him. He glanced at Jack, who was watching both of them, and he heard himself saying something he hadn't known he was going to say. "She's the kid. The one who chased us off Old Man Jennings' run years ago." He looked back at Holly, but kept speaking to Jack. "Remember her yelling at us to get off her mountain?"

Jack laughed softly at that. "Yeah, I remember."

Holly turned to Jack. "It still holds. Stay off my mountain," she said, then spun to face Cain. "And that includes you."

Cain held up one hand. "Whoa. I don't have a clue what's going on but all I did was ski one run."

He could see her gather herself, and when she spoke, her voice was level, though tight. "All he wants to take is the whole mountain."

"Get back to me later," Jack said. "Think on it. Consider the offer."

She slipped past Cain, and when she got to the door, she had her hand on the handle. "I don't have to think on it or consider the offer. There's no deal. It's not for sale." With that she left, closing the door quietly behind her.

"What in the hell was that all about?" he asked Jack.

"I want her property, and she's playing hard to get," he said as he crossed to the built-in bar. "Drink?"

"No, nothing," Cain said. "What do you want it for?"

"To expand, give the guests a tougher run. And to…" He

turned with a drink in his hand. He shrugged. "It's right behind us, and I want it."

"Like the old adage about climbing a mountain because it's there?" he asked.

Jack crossed to the couch again. "I guess so. It's great land, a fantastic run that can be developed for the guests to enjoy, and it's totally private. Perfect," he said, and sank onto the leather couch. He glanced up at Cain. "You know how great it is. You were up there this morning. I would have joined you if I'd had the time."

Cain took a seat on the opposite couch, where Holly had been sitting. He leaned forward, resting his elbows on his knees. "Why didn't you?"

"Business. About some land I own in town." He motioned toward the door with a nod. "So, she was there?"

"Yeah. She was there, at the top, mad as hell I was on her land, and wanted me to hitchhike back here."

Jack laughed at that. "You're kidding me."

"No, she was adamant about it."

"And you…?"

"I headed down the run."

Jack laughed again. "No surprise there."

"Yeah, well, I face-planted in a soft spot."

Jack guffawed, and Cain found himself joining in the laughter as Jack said, "I wish I'd seen that."

"I bet you do," Cain said.

Jack exhaled. "I remember carrying Joshua back after he wound himself around that tree on New Year's Eve."

"Well, that was a rough New Year's Eve," Cain said.

"What do you think of her?" Jack asked abruptly.

"Her?"

"Holly Winston."

So, her full name was Holly Winston. "She's a spitfire," he murmured.

"And you like that in a woman?"

Cain knew Jack and he knew him well. "Forget it, Jack. She hates me and I'm going, probably this afternoon, so forget it."

"Oh, hey, no, you can't leave so soon."

"I've got business and—"

"What about the wedding?"

"I'll fly back for it."

"What about the bachelor party?"

"You all come to the city. I'll throw a bachelor party for Joshua he'll never forget."

"He's not about to leave, and I can't."

Cain got up and went to the bar, opened a bottle of mineral water and drank a long swallow before striding over to the windows that overlooked the land around the resort. From here, you could almost make out the start of the run. Almost. The trees hid most of it. Damn, it looked straight up and down from here. "Are you going to offer her more money?" he asked.

"I'm not sure she's after more money."

"What does she want?"

"Beats me. I can't figure her out."

He turned. Jack got up, facing him across the room. "Join the club."

"What happened on the mountain?"

"Nothing." He reconsidered that. No, he'd almost done something really stupid. A kiss had been a thought, but before he could kiss her, he'd made himself stop. "She wanted me out of there, but the first time I saw her, she was angry.

Then I saw her at the school. Same thing. She stared at me as if I'm something to scrape off the bottom of her shoe."

"Oh, the old 'love-hate' ploy?" Jack asked with a partial grin.

"No, it's not 'I hate you so you'll be fascinated and run after me' at all."

The idea of her hating him was more disturbing than he'd realized until that moment. "Is she married?"

"Divorced."

Cain had the oddest idea that Holly never gave up on anything, and he wondered why she'd gotten a divorce. Teachers weren't paid well, either. None of that made sense. "She must need the money."

"She's as poor as a church mouse. She's only been back here a few weeks and is renting the old Sanders place on Eureka."

Cain remembered the house Jack was referring to. Tom Sanders had built a small bungalow on the same street as the school and the orphanage. It hadn't been fancy then, and he doubted it was fancy now. "Why won't she go for the money?"

"Well, I believe Holly Winston has her price. I just have to figure out what it is."

Anyone could be bought. Cain had found that out in his business. A price was set and either met or rejected. "Does she have any family in town?"

"Sure. Annie at the hotel. She's her sister, her half sister. The same mother, different father."

Cain drank more of his mineral water. "Do you have any idea why she'd hate me?"

Jack appeared perplexed. "What in the heck happened on the mountain?"

"Nothing." Thank goodness. He took chances, huge chances, but he hated to lose. And the idea of losing when it came to Holly Winston left an oddly bitter taste in his mouth. Maybe that was why he'd stopped any impulsive kiss on the mountain. Better not to begin in the first place. He drained the last of his water and tossed the bottle neatly into a trash container near the bar. "Absolutely nothing."

Jack didn't look convinced. "Sure, nothing," he murmured.

"Jack, don't start."

His friend shrugged. "She got to you, didn't she?"

Cain wasn't surprised that Jack had noticed whatever was going on between the two of them. "She's frustrating. I hate frustrating. I hate it when I can't figure where someone's coming from."

"How badly do you want to figure out Holly Winston?" Jack asked with the shadow of a smile playing around his lips.

He couldn't answer that, to be honest. He wanted answers about the woman, but he'd learned a long time ago to walk away from something that wasn't a sure bet. Nothing about Holly was a sure bet. He'd bet on that. He grabbed his jacket on the way to the door and tossed it over his shoulder, "I'll see you later."

"You didn't answer me," Jack called after him.

Cain paused at the door and glanced back at his friend. "Where are you going with this?" he asked.

"I just thought that if you had time to talk to her, to listen to her, you might find out why she's got an attitude about you, and in the process find out why she's hanging on to that land with such fierceness, and what it would take to have her let go." He shrugged. "But if you don't think you can do that, I'll just have to slog on and do what I can on my own."

Cain did smile then, a wry smile. "Jack, we aren't teenagers betting who can get from one end of Main Street to the other without Josh's dad catching us."

Jack shook his head. "No, we sure aren't, but a challenge is a challenge."

"Why should it be my challenge?" Cain asked, gripping the door handle.

"Why not? You're here, and you obviously see some sort of…for lack of a better word, challenge in Holly Winston. So, why not kill two birds with one stone? Get answers for both of us. Unless you don't think you're up to it."

"Jack, stop it. Just tell me what you want."

Jack stood and came over to where Cain was by the door. He stood in front of him, toe to toe. "Okay, will you talk her for me? See what you can find out, and get back to me."

A thought came to Cain. "If you're thinking of leaving Silver Creek, why do you care about that land?"

"I'm not dumping everything I worked for." Jack smiled again, a slight lift of his lips. "We're a lot alike. We both hate to lose."

Cain wouldn't argue with that. "I'm only here until tomorrow."

"Cain, I really need some help on this, and since you're here and since you're a friend, I thought…"

His voice trailed off, and Cain felt as if he were sixteen again, and the two of them were facing each other the night before he ran away from Silver Creek. Jack had realized he was going. He'd tried to talk him out of it, even said he'd get his parents to adopt Cain and make him his brother. That wouldn't have happened and they'd both accepted it, but Cain had thanked Jack and told him he was leaving, no matter what.

There had been a long silence in the darkness by the side door of the orphanage that night, broken when Jack had said, "Just tell me that you'll be back someday."

Cain had hedged, saying he would if he could, but knowing that he didn't plan on ever coming back. Jack hadn't questioned him, but shoved some money into his hand, told him to call if he could, then said, "And no matter what, if either of us needs anything, we'll be there?"

Cain had agreed to that and meant it.

To do what Jack was asking him to do now was hardly life-altering, but he found himself nodding. "Okay, if I can. If I run into her, if we talk, I'll see about getting some answers for you."

"Thanks, Cain," Jack said.

"Don't go placing any bets on me finding out anything," he said. "The odds are really long."

"And you never took long odds?"

Cain had worked the odds his whole life, and so far, he'd come out on the winning end of most bets. He wasn't sure how he'd come out if he laid any bets on Holly Winston telling him anything beyond "Get lost." But he didn't tell Jack that, simply said, "How about drinks later?"

"Sure, you and me, and I'll call Josh and Gordie."

"Good, good," he said, opened the door and strode across the outer office to the elevator.

"Hey, good luck," Jack shouted after him.

Cain hit the button for the elevator and called, "See you," before stepping into the elevator. As he turned and saw Jack at the open door, he didn't say what he was thinking: that he'd need all the luck he could get to deal with Holly Winston.

Chapter Four

Holly knew she was running away when she left the Inn. She had needed to get away from Jack and his offer just as much as she'd needed to get away from Cain Stone. She drove south toward the town and past the public ski lifts, the snow now falling more heavily. She slowed when she got near the hotel in the older part of town, but kept driving. She didn't want to see Annie just yet. The last time she'd checked, just before going in to talk to Jack, Annie had said Sierra was sleeping. She'd trust she was still sleeping, and go to the school for a while to try to work

She pulled into the parking lot of the school, the recently cleared asphalt now dusted with the new snow, and hurried out of her car, up the steps and undid the door. As it swung open, she had a flashing memory of being there with Cain standing over her—the way he'd stood over her at the ski run—and her wish that he'd drop off the face of the earth.

She went into the cold interior, stamping her boots to free them of snow, and she turned to lock the door again. But before she could swing the door shut, she was stopped by a car coming into the parking lot and pulling in beside hers. She knew the car, and she knew the man stepping out of it. He stood in the softly falling snow, looking right at her; then, without even a nod, Cain strode toward the entry.

Her first impulse was to slam the door and lock it, but that made no sense. He was no threat. What he was shouldn't be a threat to her. As he came closer, the snow clinging to his hair, she realized the threat came from her. Cain Stone, no matter what else he was, was an attractive man, with attractive eyes and an attractive smile. A man who made her tense at one glance. He was attractive, she conceded grudgingly, but she'd been so wrong when it had come to men in her life, from her father to her ex-husband, that she realized even being attractive didn't mean anything.

She heard herself speak even before she knew she'd formulated the words. "If you followed me to plead Jack Prescott's case, forget it."

He was in the doorway, the snow on his hair starting to melt and the snow on his boots spotting the tile floor underfoot. "What case are you talking about?" he asked without any anger in his voice.

"The land. My land. It's not for sale."

He was glancing past her, down the hallway, while he spoke, "That's Jack's business." he said. "I saw the door was open, and I thought that if someone was in here, I could look around a bit."

"Why?" she asked, more bluntly then she'd intended to.

His eyes narrowed on her, and she involuntarily moved a half step back. "Call it an attack of nostalgia," he said. "I haven't been back here since—"

"Yesterday," she said, cutting him off.

No anger this time, either. But a smile, a devastatingly boyish grin that totally blindsided her with its appearance.

"Yes, I was, wasn't I?" he said, then shrugged, "But this time, I thought I'd like to walk around inside the old place." His eyes never left hers. "Unless you want me out of here."

She did. That was exactly what she wanted. But she couldn't say the words. Instead, she lied. "No, of course not. Please yourself." From what she'd heard, he did what he pleased anyway.

"I will," he said, and as he came closer, she realized that her nerves were raw. She went to one side, awkwardly reaching to push the door shut behind him.

He didn't get out of her way and she bumped his arm with her shoulder. The door clanked shut, and she turned away from him. "I'm in room ten," she said over her shoulder as she headed down the hallway. "When you want to leave, tell me so I can lock up behind you." This time she knew she was running away, even if she was walking at a measured pace. She forced herself not to look back to make sure he wasn't following her.

"I'll find you," he called, his voice vaguely echoing off the metal lockers and linoleum flooring. Echoing, sort of the way it had on the mountain. She unlocked the door to her homeroom, and it was then that she allowed herself one glance back down the corridor. Watching her, Cain was where he'd stood when he'd come in, and in the empty corridor, he appeared very isolated. Unconnected. And she supposed that a man like Cain Stone didn't make connections. A man alone. A man who seemed to have everything he wanted.

She realized she'd been staring when he'd nodded to her before disappearing down the hallway that went toward the back of the school. She flicked on the lights in her room, and she was furious that her hand was less then steady. Brightness flowed into the corners of the classroom, which at thirty-by-thirty feet was large by city standards. The room was starting to feel familiar to her now. She'd hung pictures and story boards on the pale green walls. She'd repositioned the huge, old wooden desk so that she could see out the window, which overlooked the playground to her right, and see the door to her left.

She laid her purse on the desk, crossed to start the heater, then slipped off her jacket and sat down, her paperwork laid out in front of her. But she couldn't concentrate, though this time it was because she had her door open and she could hear an occasional sound echoing in the corridors. Cain moving around. Then footsteps clicking on the tiles. They got louder and closer. Then she stared at the door, waiting for him to show up.

She didn't realize she was holding her breath until he was there, and she let out a long sigh. His leather jacket was undone, and she could tell he'd raked his damp hair back with his fingers. She noticed the tan to his taut skin, the slight sharpness in his strong chin. Cain Stone, a gambler, millionaire, a hotel-casino owner and a man who had the power to destroy people's lives.

She stood as he entered her room, and she watched him glance around. "Miss Fritz," he said as he came over to where she sat at her desk. "Delphenia Fritz."

"Excuse me?"

"I was in this room for fourth grade, and my teacher was a tiny bulldozer named Delphenia Fritz. She had to be sixty, wore those god-awful black shoes that tied. And navy clothes…all her clothes were navy, buttoned to the neck, and they smelled of flowers. She had this way of regarding you as if she was sucking on lemons."

Holly could envision Delphenia Fritz. "She wasn't here when I went to school, but we had our own version—Miss Beulah Barns."

"That was easy, wasn't it?"

"What?" she asked.

He was directly opposite her with the desk between them, but she couldn't take an easy breath. "You actually smiled, sort of. At least, I think it was a smile. That's a miracle."

"That I smiled?"

"Well, when you've been looking at me as if you wished I'd drop off the face of the earth, I'd say it comes close to a miracle."

She felt the heat in her face and reached for her papers, pushed them in the folder to keep busy. Anything but meeting Cain's gaze right then. "I'm leaving. You'll have to leave, too."

"Well, you're a hell of lot prettier than Miss Fritz, but you're a bit of a bulldozer, too, aren't you?"

She grabbed her keys. "Time to go," she said, and knew damn well she wasn't smiling then.

"Yes, ma'am," he said, all but saluting as he spun on his heels and went to the open door.

As soon as he was out of sight, she put on her jacket, got her things together, then stepped out into the hallway. Cain was still there, but he wasn't watching her. He was by the windows that lined one side of the hallway, the windows that faced the front of the school and the parking lot. After she locked her room, she realized he still hadn't moved from the spot. The only movement was the slight rise of his shoulders as he took a deep breath and exhaled with a harsh sigh.

"Ready?" she asked.

He didn't meet her gaze as he said, "Sure," and went down the hallway toward the entrance. She followed, half a pace back, and he was the one to open the entry door and the one to step out first into the cold. She locked the door after him, then turned, and he was facing her, inches from her.

"Thanks for letting me look around," he said.

He seemed strained around the eyes, from tension that hadn't been there moments ago. She wasn't quite sure why she asked him, "Are you okay?"

He started doing up his leather coat. "Sure, fine, great," he said in a low voice. "I forgot how cold it could get here."

"You didn't come to talk about my land, did you?"

"Why would you think I would?"

She shrugged. "You and Jack—you were always so close. You and him, and the sheriff's kid, and Doc Gordie—you were the ones on the mountain."

He nodded. "That was us."

"I just figured that since you're so close and you were determined to ski down this morning, maybe you were in on the deal he wants, someway or another." She wasn't sure why she was saying that, except she hated games and she hated hedging. "So, I assumed—"

"Assumption is the mother of all—" He bit off his own words. "It can mess you up," he finally finished with a wry smile.

"Yes, it sure can," she said, feeling awkward standing there with him, the last person in the world she ever thought she'd have a civilized conversation with.

He hesitated, and his eyes narrowed slightly. "From the little I know about it, his offer is a fair one."

"I didn't say it wasn't."

Then he asked her something she wasn't expecting. "How

about some coffee? Or hot chocolate or some brandy or something to warm up with?"

She stared at him. Going anywhere with him was totally out of the question. "No, I can't... I..."

He held up one hand. "I just thought we could talk, and maybe you can tell me why you won't sell the land. I can try to explain it to Jack for you, if you like."

Cain's invitation was tempting. She didn't want to deal with Jack again, and if it could put an end to Jack pushing her to sell, a cup of coffee with him might be worth it. Go for coffee. That was simple, nothing complicated, in public and might end this land business once and for all. "Okay," she said.

"Good, great. We can take my car. Do you need to drop yours off somewhere?"

"No, I'll follow you," she said quickly, the idea of being in his car too unsettling for her at that moment. "I've got errands to do in town later."

He nodded and led the way down the steps. She saw him go to his car and she went for hers. She got in, started her car, then waited for him to back out and drive toward the exit before she went after him. He drove to the main street, turned north, and she was right behind him. The windows of his car were tinted, and she could barely make out his silhouette in the driver's seat. They went a few blocks and he pulled in front of Rusty's Diner, the original restaurant in Silver Creek and a very familiar place to her. At least, it had been when she was a kid.

She pulled in behind him, and by the time she got out, he was at her door, waiting for her. She exited and ducked past him to the wooden sidewalk now covered from the new snowfall. "Is this okay?" he asked as he came up by her and reached around her to push open the restaurant door.

"It's fine," she murmured, thankful for someplace familiar, someplace she felt comfortable in. Rusty's was owned by Dwayne "Rusty" Altman, who had to be around sixty-five now, and his bright red hair, which she remembered so well, had turned dusky with a gray that was echoed in his beard. Rusty had snuck her treats when she'd come in to wait for her mother to finish work as a waitress. A cookie or a muffin. She'd sit in the kitchen by the back door.

They went inside, into warmth touched with the scent of good food and wood smoke. The diner looked the same, from the heavy beams that supported the ceiling, to the rustic chandeliers that appeared to be made of antlers of some sort, to the huge deer head over the stone fireplace. The tables were partly filled, and a fire blazed in the hearth.

She'd thought she'd feel easy in here, on familiar ground, but she didn't, and she wouldn't as long as Cain was there. They crossed to an empty booth near the front windows, and a waitress she didn't recognize took their order for coffee. As she sat back and undid her jacket, she looked at Cain. He looked at ease, slipping off his leather jacket, tossing it on the seat by him in the booth. Then he glanced beyond her to the entry. "Home is where you hang your mug?" he queried.

She didn't have to glance behind her to know what he was talking about. There was a four-shelf unit by the greeting space at the doors and it held an assortment of mugs, all carefully arranged. He was reading the carved wooden sign that had been there since she was a kid: Home Is Where You Hang Your Mug.

His gaze met hers. "No one ever told me that all you needed was a mug to hang," he said with a rough chuckle.

She didn't laugh, because she was certain he wasn't feeling funny at all. Not the way his eyes narrowed and his expression tensed as he spoke. "You haven't been in here before?" she asked.

He nodded. "I was in here once, looking for a job washing dishes, but I don't remember those mugs."

Holly could imagine the tall, thin teenager trying to get work from Rusty. "They've been here forever," she said.

"Well, I came in the back door. That probably explains it."

She blinked at the tightness in his voice, and she was shocked to feel empathy for the man sitting across from her. No, for the boy he'd been. She'd heard about the orphanage, and how he'd run away. He'd been sort of a town legend among the teenage boys for a while, the one who'd broken out to live his adventures. She bet it hadn't been anything like that for him. "Did you get the job?"

"No, I didn't. I think my reputation preceded me." Cain saw her frown and he realized she didn't have a clue what he meant. "You know, as if the orphanage was like something out of Dickens. A bunch of juvenile thieves and pickpockets, taking anything that wasn't nailed down, including food, especially food."

Her eyes widened at the same time that she said, "Oh, no, it's not—"

"It is. I understood what people thought about the kids who were left there. Hell, I was lucky to have a couple of good friends and make it there as long as I did." He hated people who felt sorry for themselves, as if their pasts formed their futures and they had no say in what they became. "It doesn't matter," he said.

"Sure it does."

He expected a vague agreement that it didn't matter, but

that wasn't what she gave him. But how did she know it mattered? How could she? "What does that mean?" he asked, wary suddenly.

"When any child's treated that way, as if they're expected to do wrong or be bad, it's painful for them, really hurtful."

The waitress arrived with their coffees and he sat back while she put the mugs in front of them. But he didn't look away from Holly, or away from her expression, which was changing. He sure as hell didn't want her to go from being angry at him to being sorry for him. He'd asked Holly for coffee to talk—what Jack had asked him to do—but Cain hadn't counted on really wanting to talk to her, to not have her just walk away at the school.

Cain thought it was all about coffee and talking, but now he realized he really simply liked the idea of getting to know her better. It couldn't hurt anything, and he was finding her intriguing on some level. Coffee with an interesting woman. No, an intriguing woman. He'd done it a million times.

But even as that thought formed, he realized it was wrong. Holly didn't seem to be like the others. He'd bet there was nothing simple about her. Then she'd said what she'd said about a child being hurt. It was as if she'd known him back then, how he'd felt every time someone had glanced at him with "that look." He hadn't thought about that for what seemed forever, and he wouldn't now. He didn't need to figure out why he felt that this woman exposed something about him.

"Good coffee?" he asked, unsettled, glancing at her mug as she put it down after taking a sip.

"It's fine," she murmured, cradling the mug in her slender hands. She sighed. "I suppose you're wondering why I came for coffee with you?"

He said something off handed, something light and meant to be funny. "I thought it was because you liked my company."

That brought color to her cheeks, and now he knew that was easy to do with her. She gave away embarrassment and anger with a flush to her skin. It made her appear more delicate, made her more intriguing to him. Her amber eyes held his. "I don't know you enough to know if I'd like your company or not," she said bluntly.

"Touché," he murmured. She'd put him in his place.

"I think you were right, that maybe I can explain things to you and you can explain them to Jack."

He hadn't had to work for this at all. It had fallen into his lap, and that set him back on his heels a bit. She looked so sincere, so open, but then again, he'd been around good actresses before. Maybe she was trying to do the "I'm being totally honest with you" routine to get the price inflated even more. After all, how much could a teacher earn, especially around Silver Creek? He cut to the chase. "What price would make you part with your mountain?" he asked.

She stared at him without blinking for an unnerving minute. "There isn't a price."

"Oh, everything has a price," he said.

That expression was back in her eyes, that anger simmering in them, and her words dripped with sarcasm as she leaned forward. "You of all people would think that's true, wouldn't you?"

Her words seemed very much at odds with the happy Christmas music being piped into the restaurant and the laughter of other customers over by the stone fireplace. The words were harsh and condemning. "I'm like anyone else," he said, trying to get his footing with her. "Money helps everything, one way or another."

She looked away from him, picked up the mug and took a small sip. He could see her knuckles whiten as she gripped the mug. "I'd expect you to say that," she said tightly.

His own anger was starting to grow. "Oh, you're above money? You have so much that you don't need more?" he asked with his own tinge of sarcasm.

He almost thought she flinched, then she simply let go of her mug and said in a low voice, "No, I don't have much money."

He sat forward, ignoring his coffee. "Then why don't you want to take Jack's offer for the mountain?"

He wasn't sure what he had expected her to reply, but it wasn't what she said. "It was my father's and now it's mine. To keep it. To hold on to it. To not let it go."

He sat back, cupping his mug between his hands, but he never took his eyes off Holly. He had never had family, so it was impossible for him to figure out why, just because it was her father's, Holly wouldn't take the money. The man, as far as he remembered Jennings, had been a drunk and a trouble-maker, and pretty much hated by the town in general. Hardly the memories one would want to keep at the loss of a great deal of money. "You've got plans for it?" he asked, suddenly wondering if someone else wasn't going in with her on developing that land. If that was the case, it would certainly put a crimp in the privacy at the Inn and cut into the Inn's profits.

"No."

The single word hung between them. "You're not going to build on it, or anything?"

She actually smiled at that. "Build? No. There's the cabin on the land. I won't be building anything else."

"Why not?" He really didn't understand at all.

She shrugged, a fluttery motion of her shoulders. "The time I had with my father was there, and it's a sturdy cabin. It's useable."

He wanted to understand. "The times with your father were that good for you?"

That brought a bit of color to her cheeks and she looked down at her all-but-forgotten coffee mug. "No, they weren't good, not usually," she said in a low voice almost drowned out by the Christmas music.

"Then why keep the place?"

"My father—well, you know how he was. The town said he was eccentric, at best, and my mother said he was a bum. I'd go to see him at the cabin every week or two. At first, I was so young there wasn't anything to do except watch him drink. Then I started skiing, and one day he was really doing badly and I decided to go skiing for a while. I found the run there, and it was wonderful." She finally looked up at him, and her expression was vaguely sad, but also there was an expression in her eyes that he understood. "Taking off from the top, sailing down, free, nothing but me and mountain." She blushed. "I'm not a great skier, but it was a place I found that was all mine, and I'd peer down at Silver Creek from up there, and the world seemed in balance, even if it wasn't." She bit her lip. "Never mind. That's not important. What's important is, I'm not giving it up."

In that moment, he realized he'd done what he never thought he would. He understood Holly Winston—at least, one small part of her. "I understand," he said.

She frowned. "No, you don't. Even my own sister doesn't." She scrambled out of the booth, and he found himself looking up at her as she buttoned her jacket and said, "The bottom line is, it's not for sale." She grabbed her purse from the seat. "Tell Jack that for me, okay?"

He'd never realized that anyone else had those feelings about the run and he didn't want Holly to walk away like this. "Sit down. Finish your coffee and we can talk some more."

She glanced at the cup, then back at him. "I'm done," she murmured, and turned to leave.

Cain tossed some bills onto the table and went after her. He stepped out into the snow of the gray day and caught up to her at her car. "Holly?" he said.

He saw her hesitate, then turn back to him. Her face lifted to his, and the snow brushed her skin. Her lips were softly parted in question, and for a moment, he was rocked by a thought so outrageous that it was barely containable. He wanted to touch her. He wanted to stroke her cheek free of snow, then taste her lips. Make a connection with her the way he'd felt it when she'd talked about the skiing being her freedom. That last idea drove him to push his hands deep in the pockets of his leather coat. He was never a man who shared much with others, but right then he wanted to find a quiet place and tell Holly about his last day on the mountain, the day before he'd run away.

"I was wondering if maybe—" he started to say, but his question about them maybe seeing each other again was cut off when someone called out to Holly.

He went toward the voice and saw Annie from the hotel, hurrying up the street toward them with a small child in tow. "Holly, I thought that was your car." She slowed as she approached and saw him there. "Cain? I heard you were back."

He nodded to her. "For a few days," he said.

She glanced from him to Holly, then back to him again. "Are we interrupting something?"

"No," Holly said, and turned from Cain. The next thing he knew, she had the child in her arms, and the child was holding on to her tight, huge blue eyes staring at Cain. It was then that he realized the little girl had red hair and translucent skin. "Cain, this is my daughter, Sierra." She was a miniature of her mother, but with blue eyes instead of amber.

A child. The idea of getting together with Holly again while he was here vanished. It had been self-indulgent, anyway. He already had Jack's information. He'd never talk to her about the runs on the mountain, the days he'd stolen up there to be free, to just let go. He wouldn't tell her anything, and that was for the best. He nodded to Holly and her child. "I need to go," he said, and realized his words were abrupt. He glanced at Annie, said, "Good to see you again," then headed to his car.

He got in, barely glanced back at them as he turned on the motor and drove out onto the street. Cain had known from the start that he'd never do "family," in any shape or form. Had never wanted to. And Holly Winston was very "family," with a child, a sister and a father who had been no good but still held on to her in some way. He headed north and didn't glance back.

Chapter Five

Holly knew she should have been relieved when Cain left, but she couldn't explain a definite sense of disappointment as he drove out of sight. She didn't understand why she'd told him about her father and the mountain. It was nothing to him. And he was nothing to her. She just didn't understand why she'd opened up to him. She hadn't talked to anyone about the mountain except for Annie, and she hadn't even told Annie what she'd told Cain.

"Mama," Sierra said, more on a whine than anything, and Holly could tell her daughter was tired. She put her head on Holly's shoulder and her thumb found her mouth.

Holly patted her back and looked over at Annie. "I'll get her home."

She set Sierra in her car seat in the back of the car, then closed the door and turned to Annie. "Thanks for keeping her. I meant to get back sooner, but I had things to do."

"Things to do? Did you come out of Rusty's with Cain?"

"We had coffee."

Annie appeared shocked. "Holly, you had coffee with him and you're always telling me that you hate him?"

Holly almost said she did hate him, but she stopped.

Hate wasn't the word, not anymore. She shrugged. "I just thought he could explain to Jack why the land isn't for sale."

"When he explains it to Jack, send him on over to the hotel to explain it to me," Annie said.

"Oh, Annie," Holly said on a sigh, weary with people not understanding what she was doing.

"I know, I know. You want to keep it."

"For Sierra and for me."

Annie smiled, but it wasn't a particularly happy expression. It had a touch of sadness. "Of course. It's important to you."

"It's my connection and Sierra's, to the past, to my roots. I can't imagine not having the mountain to go to."

Annie had never liked skiing and she had only been at the cabin a few times in all the years Holly lived in Silver Creek. She probably thought it was tiny and worn and depressing. "You don't have to do anything right away. You've made enough decisions for now."

"Thanks," Holly said softly, then added with more enthusiasm, "Thanks for taking care of Sierra."

Annie's smile was still sad, but in a different way. "I love watching her. I wish…" Her voice trailed off. Annie had never been able to have children, and Sierra was benefiting from all that maternal instinct that had no where to go except to the occupants of Annie's hotel and a favorite niece. "I'll see you tomorrow," she said.

"Yeah," Holly said, gave her sister a hug, then got in the car with her daughter and headed home.

The small house was frigid when Holly walked in with Sierra in her arms. The child didn't seem to notice. She wiggled out of Holly's arms and ran off full tilt for her room.

Holly laid wood in the hearth and started the fire, then got out of her outer clothes and finally sighed heavily.

She glanced around the living room, at the old furniture that had come with the rental, the couch and two chairs that were showing their age, with threadbare arms and pillows that would never plump up again. The small coffee table and end tables were scarred, and the worn hardwood floors were only partially covered by a faded braided rug. The fireplace was her favorite thing. All stone and too big for the space, it worked well, spilling heat out into the room.

She stared at the wood as it crackled to life and felt the heat begin to radiate from it. A fireplace heated the old cabin, too, and she remembered the smell of wood smoke in the chilly air, the way the flames flickered from the fires her father built. How she'd add kindling; then, as she'd gotten older, had put in split logs to keep the cabin reasonably warm when she'd be leaving and her father would be passed out.

She turned from the fireplace, closing her eyes, not wanting to dwell on those years, but a piece of that past came to her right then. It startled her that she could almost see Cain as a teenager at the top of the run, taking off before her father got to him, then Cain as a man, toe to toe with her at the top of the run. Cain facedown in the snow. Cain laughing up at her as he got to his feet. Cain across the table from her at the diner, listening to things she never should have told him.

Cain Stone. The man who had let Travis lose everything. That truth brought it all back into focus. If she remembered anything, that would be it. Going to the Dream Catcher, trying to get Travis to leave, being told it wasn't casino policy to stop anyone from making bets, no matter what the situation, short of criminal activity. That was why they were in business, one security boss had told her. Money. Period. And Travis had their money—at least, until he'd lost everything.

She clutched at that anger, but had trouble holding on to it and reconciling it with the man she'd found on the mountain. A man who smiled, who didn't like fancy coffee. A man who stirred sympathy in her, even made her feel sorry for the boy he must have been.

A shriek of laughter from Sierra's room, then a thumping sound, startled her and she ran into her daughter's room. A wooden block had made the thump and thankfully hadn't done any damage. She picked it up, then sat on the floor with Sierra and started stacking blocks. One by one. Anything to just not think for a while. The phone rang three times while the two of them played, and each time Holly checked the caller ID. It showed the number for the Inn. Cain had probably talked to Jack by now, and it hadn't done a bit of good. Jack was calling to keep at her. She made a mental note to get an answering machine as soon as she could and went back to playing with Sierra.

Two hours later, the house was calm, Sierra was napping and blocks had finally been picked up and put away. Holly put another log on the fire, and was startled when the phone by her on the end table rang. She checked the ID, and was relieved to see the number for her sister's hotel.

"Hi, Annie," she said as she answered it.

"Guess what?" Annie said, definitely excited.

"What?"

"A Mr. Malone called me just a minute ago, and you'll never guess what he said."

She didn't know a Mr. Malone. "Who's Mr. Malone?"

"Jack Prescott's assistant."

The big man she'd met at the Inn. The single-named man, Malone. She grew cautious. She was sure she'd been right. Cain had spoken to Jack and Jack hadn't accepted her decision. Not only that, now he was trying to reach her through Annie. "Annie, I don't want you getting in the middle of my discussions with Jack about the mountain."

"Oh, honey, I'm not," she said quickly. "It didn't come up. And the only reason he phoned me was that you weren't answering your phone."

So he'd gone to her sister. "It's not any of your business."

"It's not about the land. He actually called to ask us all to the Inn tonight for their Santa sighting. Jack remembered that you had a child, and thought Sierra might like to see Santa 'up close and personal,' as Mr. Malone said. They do it every year. I've heard about, but I never dreamed we'd get to go to it."

She couldn't stop a heavy sigh. "Annie, this isn't out of the goodness of his heart, and he's—"

"Holly, I'm not dense," Annie said. "I know what he's up to. But my thought is, Sierra would love to meet Santa in person, and we could all use some fun, and I've heard about these parties. Besides, I've got the hotel covered for the night. Darren's staying, so why not take advantage of it, and say thank-you, have some fun for a change and walk away? Mr. Malone mentioned that there's a dinner, and caroling and presents."

Holly could hear the excitement in Annie's voice, and she knew her sister didn't do much for herself. She ran the hotel and worried about everyone else in her world. Holly didn't want to go to the Inn again, period, but she found herself cautiously agreeing. "You really think it's a good idea."

"I think it'll be the first time we've had a time out together in ages, and Sierra will love it."

Holly would let it be that simple. Something for Annie. Something for Sierra. She was three, an age where Santa was the best thing going. "Sierra is crazy for Santa."

"Then you'll do it?"

"Okay. We'll go, and you can head off Mr. Prescott when he swoops in for the kill."

Annie giggled like a teenager. "I'll be glad to head off Jack. No problem."

"Okay then, we'll do it."

"Great! I'll call Mr. Malone and tell him we're coming. It's at six for the Santa party, then dinner afterward. Rick and I'll pick you up at five-thirty. Okay?"

"Sure, fine," she said, and hung up.

Holly glanced at the clock by the fireplace. She had two hours to get ready, and she had no idea how anyone dressed for a party at the Inn. Then she decided it didn't matter. She'd wear what she had. By the time Annie and Rick arrived to pick up her and Sierra, Holly was dressed in an emerald-green sweater with a cowl neckline, and black slacks. She found a pair of black suede boots and put them with her purse, then stepped into her snow boots and navy jacket. She left her hair down, but pulled it back off her face with a pair of gold clips that Annie had given her years ago.

Sierra bounced around the living room, chanting incessantly, "Going to see Santa, Santa, Santa." The little girl was a bright picture in a red sweater with a Santa knit into it on the front, worn with white leggings and green boots. Her carroty hair was done in two braids trimmed with green ribbons, and her face was wreathed in smiles. "Santa, Santa," she kept saying when Rick and Annie loaded her into their car.

The four of them got through the entry gates at the resort

with just a word to the guard. As they approached the main lodge, its lights blazing in the snowy night, the sounds of music could be heard faintly. They drove Rick's old four-wheel-drive vehicle up to the entrance, and a valet was there right away. Holly took off her snow boots, slipped on her suede ones; then, hugging her old jacket around her, she got out. Rick carried Sierra as they went up the steps.

Holly had never come in the main doors to the Inn before, and if she'd been impressed by Jack's private quarters, she was nearly stunned at the space in front of her. Vaulted ceilings soared twenty feet above a smoothly polished stone floor. A reception desk that took up one full section of the back wall looked fashioned from stone. Chairs were grouped everywhere to take advantage of a fireplace that stood dead center in the space.

The fireplace was built from river stones, and it rose up through the soaring beamed ceiling. It had been built so the fire could be enjoyed on all sides. People grouped around it, some drinking, some resting and some just watching the blaze. She was relieved to see that everyone was in skiing clothes of one type or another. No fancy gowns or suits.

To the right, under stained glass windows, sat the biggest Christmas tree Holly had ever seen. It was decorated in gold and green, and almost touched the ceiling with its topping star. Lights twinkled in its branches and the scents of wood smoke and pine perfumed in the air.

"Holy cow," Annie breathed at her side. "So, this is the way the other half lives."

"I guess it is," Holly said, watching Rick put Sierra down.

She reached to grab her daughter's hand just before Sierra was about to take off for the tree.

"Good evening," someone to her left said. She turned with Sierra firmly in tow to find Jack's assistant standing there. The big man was about the only one dressed in a suit, an all black suit, worn with a black shirt and silver tie. He had to be six-foot two or three, with steel-gray hair cut close to his scalp, a barrel chest and deeply tanned skin. His pale gray eyes were startling in his lined face. "I'm Malone," he said in a deep bass voice that matched his build. He held out a hand to each of them, and when he took Holly's in his, his hand dwarfed hers. "Mr. Prescott said to make sure you were all comfortable and had a good time."

Annie laughed slightly. "Wow, this is great. I'm Annie, the one you spoke to, and this is my husband, Rick, and this is my sister, Holly."

Malone nodded at Annie and Rick, then at Holly. "Nice to see you again," he murmured, then smiled as he looked down at Sierra. "Well, hello, missy," he said, and crouched in front of her. "Did they tell you that Santa Claus is coming to the Inn tonight?"

"Huh!" Sierra said, bobbing her head so enthusiastically that her braids bounced around her face. "Santa's coming."

"And you're just in time." He leaned a bit closer and whispered conspiratorially, "I think someone heard jingling bells on the roof a few minutes ago."

Sierra's eye grew large with wonder, and Holly knew she'd done the right thing in coming here with her. "Really?"

"That's the word," the big man said, then tapped her nose with the tip of his forefinger and stood. "They're having the Santa party in our banquet room," he said, and led the four of them toward the reception desk. He veered off into a broad hallway done in deep, rich cherrywood walls. His voice echoed slightly when he spoke as he approached two massive wooden doors framed with holly and tinsel. An intricate sign on them read Santa's Party.

"We're going in here. I have your seats all ready for you," he said, and reached to pull the nearest door open.

Music and the sounds of children laughing spilled out into the hallway. Sierra all but tugged Holly into the room with her, bouncing from excitement as she took in the wonder in front of her. The space was huge, and filled with children and their parents. Red and green streamers decorated the beamed ceiling and a Christmas tree done in red and gold ribbons, along with small presents on each branch, dominated the middle of the room.

Chairs four-deep circled the tree, and huge flat-screen TVs hung on each wall, all showing an assortment of Christmas cartoons. Malone led them through the partyers to a table near the tree and a gold throne that sat on a raised platform under an arch of mistletoe. He plucked the Reserved placard off a small bouquet of candy canes in the middle of the table, then turned to help Sierra get into one of the chairs.

Holly sat by Sierra, and Malone leaned down toward her so she could hear him over the noise. "Santa will be right in. After Santa's appearance, there's a little show, then gift giving. I'll be back to take you to dinner in the Eagle's Nest."

She didn't have a clue what the Eagle's Nest was, but she nodded, and he slipped away. She glanced at Sierra, who seemed stunned by the splendor of her surroundings. She glanced at Annie, who looked almost as in awe as her niece. "Wow, this is like a kid's dream come true. And the Eagle's Nest," Annie said. "I've heard the food there is fantastic."

Right then, Holly was glad Annie had talked her into this.

She didn't owe Jack anything. She'd accept this as a gift, one she'd been able to share with Sierra and Annie. There was a trumpet sound, then the doors opened, and as music began, Santa entered. Not just any Santa, but a Santa who could have been real. He wasn't Charlie Sloan, the sheriff, in the costume. This Santa did a wonderful "Ho-ho," as he smiled and waved to the kids, and he actually had rosy cheeks and a belly that shook "like a bowlful of jelly." He was perfect.

An hour later, Santa was gone and Sierra was on Holly's lap, examining the doll that had been in the wrapped present Santa had given her with her name on it. Annie leaned close to Sierra. "Wow, Santa looked terrific, didn't he, kiddo?"

Sierra smiled up at her aunt. "Terrific," she echoed.

"I can't wait to see what they have for dinner," Annie said to Holly as she patted Sierra's head.

"We've enjoyed this, and maybe it's time to go."

Annie frowned. "Oh, come on." She leaned closer to half whisper to Holly. "If Jack Prescott wants to bribe you, let him. It's too bad he doesn't know you, and that you're as stubborn as hell when you want to be. But that doesn't mean we can't enjoy this and have a great meal."

She sighed. "Okay, okay."

Annie moved back and grinned at her. "Good girl."

Malone was there, bending over Holly. "Ma'am, Mr. Prescott arranged to have a personal sitter keep your daughter and get her dinner while you all enjoy your meal."

A sitter? "Oh, no, I don't—"

"If you're worried, let me assure you that Louise Shane is a very good with children and—"

"Louise Shane?" Annie said, looking at Holly. "I forgot she works here. You remember Louise Allan?" Holly had to think for a minute; then, when Annie said, "She dated Clint Shane around the time Rick and I got married," she knew who Annie meant.

"Oh, sure."

"She'll be wonderful with Sierra. She's really sweet."

Holly stood, gathering Sierra up in her arms, doll and all. "I guess that would be okay, but I want to stay with her for a few minutes," she said to Malone. "I can't just leave her with a stranger."

"Ma'am, she'll be fine, and your reservations at the Eagle's Nest—"

Annie cut in to say, "Why don't you go in and settle her, Holly, and we'll head to the restaurant to get our table. When you feel it's okay, come and meet us there. I'll order drinks and appetizers, and we'll wait for you."

Holly looked at Malone. "I don't suppose the restaurant is set up for kids."

He shook his head. "No, ma'am. It's really not."

She looked at Annie and Rick. "I'll meet you two in a bit."

Annie and Rick left, and Malone touched Holly's arm. "I'll take you to Louise."

CAIN WAS LEAVING. He'd told Jack he'd be back for the wedding, but until then he was returning to Vegas to work. He'd locked up his cabin and was driving his car toward the gates, when he spotted Jack at the side entry to the main lodge. Jack was in his outer clothes, talking to the man who ran the lifts. Harvey something-or-other, he thought, and they were in an animated discussion about something. He would have driven right past, but Jack spotted him in the glow of the lanterns that lined the drives at the Inn and waved him down.

Cain stopped, rolled down his window and peered out. "What's going on?"

Jack crossed to Cain's car. "I've got trouble. The main lift burned out a gear, and Harvey's giving me grief about having to bring in a crew for overtime. Malone's not answering the page, and I've got to get to the lift to figure this out."

Cain waited for whatever it was that Jack was asking him to do before he took off. "And?"

"Could you run in and find Malone? He's somewhere around the banquet area, keeping tabs on—" He shrugged. "He's busy. Tell him I need him to call lift maintenance and find out when they can get their own crew out here."

Cain glanced at the clock. Seven. It didn't matter how late he arrived in Las Vegas, and it was only a three-hour drive. "Okay, I'll find him for you," he said.

Jack waved him to the parking area by the side door. "Thanks, I owe you."

"Sure you do," Cain murmured, and drove over to the slot by the door. He turned off his car, got out and waved to Jack, then hurried up the steps and ducked into the lodge.

He had barely gone past the private elevator entrance in the corridor, when he spotted Malone. But the big man wasn't alone. Cain stopped when he realized the man was with Holly. The sight of her in a deep green sweater, clinging dark slacks and square-heeled boots that did nothing to equalize her height with the big man beside her made his middle tighten. Her hair fell free around her shoulders but was swept back at her temples by sparkling clips, and she had her daughter in her arms. Malone was at her elbow, guiding her across the hallway to another set of doors. He pulled one open for her, then waited for her to go inside before he followed and the door closed behind them.

Cain was still for a very long moment, trying to figure out what had just happened to him. Whatever he'd felt stir in him before around Holly came back with a life of its own. Living in Las Vegas, he'd seen beautiful women of every type, and he thought he'd become immune to being stunned by the sight of them. But at that instant, his glimpse of Holly had rocked his world. He hadn't expected it, not when he'd written it all off the time she'd introduced her daughter to him. He was smart enough and honest enough to know that even if he was attracted to her, which he was, she had a child and that put her out of his realm of reality.

He moved toward the door, thinking he'd step inside and catch Malone's attention, then get out of town. He reached to ease the door back enough to look into the room beyond. It was a child's play area, probably part of the child care Jack provided for his guests and their children. Toys were everywhere, from playhouses to rocking horses to blocks and balls and castles and a nursery. Holly stood in the middle of the room with her back to the door, Malone at her side, her daughter in her arms. He heard her saying, "I'm not sure at all."

Then he saw Louise. He couldn't remember her last name, but she'd gone to school with them. He did remember her being nicer than some of the other kids, a quiet girl who seemed a born nurturer. Louise was a plain woman, with dark hair and glasses. She wore a Christmas sweater, with a huge silver star knitted into it, worn with red tights. He thought she had on pixie boots, with bells on the toes, but didn't know for sure until she moved closer to Holly and the child and he heard the bells jingle.

"We'll have a great time, and…" She held something out to Holly. "Here's a pager, and if there happens to be a problem, anything at all, I'll page you."

Holly hesitated, then reached for the pager with one hand while Louise spoke to the child. "How about coming to my dollhouse and helping me set up the furniture."

The child seemed to hold back, then shifted, letting Louise take her from Holly. There was a moment when her expression pulled into a frown until Louise said, "I'll let you put up the Christmas tree in the dollhouse."

That brought a smile, and Holly spoke up. "Okay, I'll just get her settled before I leave."

"Of course," Louise said as Malone leaned toward Holly and said something, nodded and turned to leave.

Cain let go of the door and stood back. The next moment, the door moved again and Malone was there. He saw Cain. "Good evening, sir."

"There's a problem at the main lift. Jack asked me to find you and have you get up to the office and contact lift maintenance. Find out how soon they can bring a crew out here."

Malone didn't pose any questions. "I'll get right on it," he said. "Mrs. Winston's in the playroom. When she comes out, could you tell her that I'll meet up with her later? She's to go to the Eagle's Nest to meet her family there. Klaus knows all about it."

"Sure," Cain said, and the big man took off for the elevator.

Before Cain could go inside, Holly was slipping out into the hallway. Whatever had happened when he'd first spotted her in the hallway was there again, tightening his body and making him overly aware of the fullness of her bottom lip, the deep amber of her eyes and the way the air stirred with a scent that reminded him of flowers and softness.

When she looked up and saw him, those amber eyes widened then ridiculously long lashes lowered slightly and she turned as if she was going to go in the opposite direction. "Holly?" he said, and she turned back to him.

"What are you doing here?" she asked in a low voice, clutching a small black purse to her middle with both hands as her finely etched eyebrows tugged into that frown again.

"Waiting for you." The words were unintentionally suggestive, and he could see the color rise in her face.

"Excuse me?"

He spoke quickly. "Malone asked me to let you know that he had to take care of some business, and that he'd catch up."

"Oh, okay," she said. "Thanks."

Then he embellished on Malone's request, something for himself. He had time. "He also asked me to make sure you got to the restaurant."

He didn't miss her inhaling a deep breath, an action that lifted the breasts under her jewel-toned sweater. The tightness in him wasn't easing. "So, you're supposed to babysit me now?"

He blinked. Babysitting was the last thing on his mind. "What?"

"Let's make this simple. I'll find the restaurant, and you go and tell Jack that I'm there. When Malone shows up, I'll tell him that I had a lovely time." She hesitated. "You did pass on my message to Jack, didn't you?"

"I did." Jack had listened, said he was impressed that she'd opened up to Cain, that he wouldn't ask Cain what he'd done to make her open up to him. Before Cain had been able to explain, Jack had said, "Okay, I'll have to try something else."

"I thought so." She sighed. "He just won't accept no for an answer." She looked directly at him. "The land isn't for sale."

He found himself smiling at her bluntness. "I pretty much figured that one out."

"You're smarter than he is," she murmured, and he wondered if he might be seeing the suggestion of a smile playing around her lips, pushing away the frown. He liked that idea. He liked it a lot.

"This is all wasted?" he asked, motioning vaguely to their surroundings.

"No, what's a waste when he provided Santa? Sierra was thrilled and Annie and Rick are enjoying themselves. It was a win-win situation for me."

He really wished the smile would break through. "So, you came, you saw, you had fun and you're keeping your mountain."

If a smile had been coming, it was gone now. The frown was back. "Now, I need to get to the Eagle's Nest, find Annie and Rick and have this fantastic dinner while Sierra gets to play with one of the most terrific dollhouses I've ever seen." She glanced around, then down the hall toward the main area of the lodge. "Just point me in the right direction, and I'm all set."

He wasn't ready to stop this, not yet. The prospect of her smiling had cemented that idea. "I'll take you," he said, and before she could object, he didn't miss a beat adding a lie of his own. "I happened to be on my way to the Eagle's Nest."

Chapter Six

Holly stared at Cain—at the deep blue eyes; at the way his hair was slightly mussed as if he'd run his fingers through it; at that leather jacket he had on, open to show a simple gray sweater worn with dark slacks. Why did a man like him have to be so damn attractive, and so damn persistent and so dangerous for her? He was babysitting. She knew it, but didn't fight it.

But before she could agree to anything, a young guy with long blond hair, dressed all in green, approached. "Ms. Winston?" he asked.

She nodded. "Yes."

He held out a folded piece of paper. "This is for you."

One more thing from Jack Prescott? She took the paper, opened it and saw Annie's neat script on the ivory stationery of the Inn.

Sorry, we had to leave. Stay and enjoy. Call when you and Sierra are ready to come home so Rick can pick you up. Love, A.

She looked at the young man. "When did she give you this?"

"I don't know. Klaus asked me to deliver it and to find out when you'd be ready to be seated for dinner."

"Tell him I won't be there," she said, and with a nod the man left.

"What's wrong?" Cain asked.

"Annie and Rick have gone. Probably an emergency at the hotel or something." She pushed the note into her purse.

"You're not staying?"

"No. This was all Annie's idea in the first place, and Sierra got her Santa fix. It's time to go. I just have to find a house phone."

"Why not stay and have dinner with me?" Cain proposed.

She met his blue eyes as the words hung between them. A simple invitation, but impossible. No, she shouldn't be here. Shouldn't be around him. "Oh, no," she said, and realized her reply had been too abrupt when he frowned. "Listen, you don't have to do this. Tell Jack I had a lovely time, and I'm going home. I don't require a babysitter, or you to try to convince me that the Inn has to have my mountain."

"I asked you for dinner, not for a sales pitch," he murmured.

The idea of sitting with him, just the two of them, over wine and food, was unnerving at best. "Thanks, but no." She would have gone back inside to get Sierra, but his hand circled her upper arm and kept her from moving.

She took a breath, braced herself and turned, thankfully feeling his touch leave her. "What do you need now?" she asked, not about to apologize for the tone of her voice.

He uttered a low expletive that made her flinch, and she saw real anger in his face. "Forget it. I'm heading back to Las Vegas, but before I go, I want to know one thing."

She pulled her purse to her middle to press against a spreading ache in her stomach. "What?"

"Why do you hate me so much?"

Hate? God help her, it wasn't hate. She guessed it never had been. If she hated anyone, it wasn't him. She hated herself. She was the one who'd believed Travis. She was the one who'd let him take everything she had. She was the one who'd stood there while he'd lost everything. She looked down, closing her eyes. "Please, just—"

She never finished. He touched her again, this time cupping her chin and lifting her face until she had no choice but to open her eyes and look up at him. "Why?" he whispered roughly.

She twisted her head, freeing herself. "Stop this."

But he didn't. "Why?" he repeated again, but this time there was no touch. Just him in front of her, not moving, saying, "What did I ever do to you?"

Words were there, boiling up in her, words that had festered for the past year. Then they were there between them, said and never to be taken back. "Because you destroyed my life."

Cain stared at her for a long, agonizing moment, then uttered, "What in the hell are you talking about?"

Her heart was hammering against her ribs and she glanced away from Cain. She wished with all her heart that she had never said that. She wished with all her heart that Cain weren't there. She wished with all her heart that she'd never come tonight. "I'm sorry," she said. "I have to go."

"No."

The single word riveted her to the spot, and she was having trouble even breathing in a regular pattern. "I can't—"

Cain shut off her protest by clasping her upper arm, and through the soft wool of her sweater, she could feel the grip of his fingers. "Of course you can stay," he said in a low voice. "You owe me an explanation." He glanced around, then said, "In there," motioning to the banquet room where the party had been held. "We can talk in there."

She thought of digging in her heels, but rejected that course of action. Short of making him drag her, she couldn't fight his hold on her, and in fact, she had to admit that he deserved an explanation of some sort. She just wasn't at all sure she could give him one with any coherency. But she went with him, toward the closed doors, and pulled out of his grasp as he pushed back the closest door. She ducked past him into the room, which was empty now.

The cleanup crew hadn't been there yet, and the remnants of the party still littered the huge space. Cain touched her shoulder, and when she looked at him, he pointed to the back area, to a smaller room. "Over there," he said.

She went ahead of him, toward the other space, and stepped into what had probably been used as a bar area at adult parties, but today had been used to store the gifts. Two chairs by a set of back windows gave a view of the ski lifts, and she headed for the nearest one. Her legs weren't all that steady, and she was grateful to sit onto the red plaid fabric of the wing chair.

She dropped her purse by her on the seat, then hugged her arms around herself, cold despite the heat in the room. Then Cain was opposite her in the other chair, separated by a mere two feet of space. If she moved her feet, her boots would kick his. She tucked her feet under her chair and finally met his gaze.

The lights emphasized the hollow at his throat and the tightness of his expression. On top of everything else, she found it hard to breathe and she felt dizzy.

"Okay, explain," he said, sitting forward, robbing her of any cushion of space between them. His elbows rested on his knees and his hands were clasped together. "You hate me because I destroyed your life?"

Right then there was pain and sadness, great sadness for both her and Sierra. But no hate, and she almost felt as if she'd been cut adrift. She'd clutched at that hate for so very long. "I don't hate you," she whispered, her voice so low that Cain frowned at her.

"What?" he asked.

"I don't hate you," she said more loudly, and for a moment her words echoed in the smaller space. She sank into her chair and shrugged. "I don't hate you," she said again, flatness in her tone. She didn't have that to hold around her any longer. She didn't have it as a crutch to keep her going. Now she had only the truth. She'd let it all happen, and before she'd met Cain, blaming him for things had been so easy. Now she couldn't. She and she alone had been responsible for where her life had gone.

"If someone destroyed my life, I'd hate him," Cain murmured, his eyes never leaving hers. "But I don't even know you. I can't understand how I could have a thing to do with what happened in your life."

"I know," she breathed, and wished she had something to drink to settle her down. "It wasn't you but what you are, I guess," she said, and realized that she was only making this worse.

He stared at her hard. "How could anything I am destroy your life?"

"Please, this is ridiculous." She sounded as panicked as she felt. "I just need to go. Forget I said anything. It doesn't matter, not at all, not anymore."

"You bet it does," he contradicted her, and the harshness in his tone almost made her flinch. "You know, all my life people have accused me of things that they thought I did. At the start. Back at the orphanage, on through the rest of my life." His eyes narrowed on her. "I hate the idea of you doing that. I really hate it."

She did flinch then. "So we're even, aren't we?" She heard her own voice, but it sounded distant and odd to her.

"Oh, you hate me, I hate you, even Steven?"

"That's ridiculous," she managed to get out.

"Yeah, it is, isn't it?" He laughed at that, a rough, humorless laugh. In his eyes, there was something she almost thought was pain. Then he lowered his lashes and everything was hidden except the roughness in his voice.

"Growing up at the orphanage, I thought I got used to people thinking the worst of me. But this…" He shrugged sharply. "Forget it," he muttered. "Just forget it."

Cain stood, towering over her for a moment, then he moved away, and she was free to go. She knew it. Just had to get up and leave, and she'd never see Cain again. But she couldn't do it.

For some reason, the idea of just walking away wasn't an option for her after all. She looked at him, his back to her as he looked out the windows. "It was horrible at the orphanage, wasn't it?"

He didn't respond at all for so long that she thought she'd only imagined saying the words. Then he finally turned, and she knew he'd heard her. "It wasn't like something out of *Little Orphan Annie*, but it was okay. The couple who ran it really tried to make things okay for the kids." He pushed back the sides of his jacket and tucked the tips of his fingers in the pockets of his dark slacks. "But they only had so much time, energy and money. When I left, it probably helped some of the other kids."

She couldn't take her eyes off him, the words coming out as if he was talking about the weather, yet they caught at her heart. He believed his leaving helped other kids? "When did you run away?"

"I was about sixteen. I decided it was time. I had no ties there or anywhere and the whole world was waiting." He smiled ruefully. "I went out to meet it."

She'd never thought about a child who had no one, going out into the world. "I went out to meet it" sounded grand and brave, but she had to believe that a kid wouldn't have felt terribly brave at all heading out alone. "Where were you going to go?"

He came back to the chair and dropped into it to face her, clasping his hands on his stomach and regarding her from under lowered lids. "Nowhere special. I took off one morning, right after I made one more cut down your mountain for the last time. I just kept going for a very long time. I was in Mississippi for a while, up in New York, but it got so damn cold there I left after I had a run-in with the local school authorities. They frowned on me working and not getting educated. So, I headed south again, to Texas. I did a bit of everything." He ran a hand over his face, then reclasped his hands on his stomach. "One day, I realized that I was good at one thing. Damn good at it. I got into a poker game with some older guys at an oil rig I was working on, and I took the pot. The next time, I won again." He smiled that rueful smile again. "I do believe they thought I was cheating."

"Were you?"

He didn't seem offended by her question. "Hell, no, I never had to. I don't know if it was luck or skill, but I had a way with cards. I knew when to hold them and when to fold them. They believed I was taking huge chances, but the fact is, I had hunches, and it was instinct when to bet and when not to bet." He shifted, resting his hands on the arms of the chair now. "I ended up in Las Vegas, got a job busing in one of the casinos on the Strip, and one night, I found myself in a closed game."

"What's that?" she asked.

"You get in by invitation only, a matter of who you know. I got to be friends with a guy on the inside, and he got me in. It changed my life. I started playing regularly with some really big hitters and usually won. After a while, I ended up in a game where shares of the Dream Catcher were in the pot. I won, got involved and eventually bought out the others." He shrugged. "The rest, as they say, is history."

He'd given her a brief bio of a gambler, a man whose life was built on luck, the turn of the card, the luck of the draw. The way her ex-husband's was, except Cain had good luck. Travis never had any luck except bad luck. She realized that Cain hadn't mentioned a thing about his personal life. "That sounds like a résumé," she said.

He looked taken aback for a moment. "I guess it does. But there isn't much else. I like the color red, can't stand sour cream and prefer day to night. I've never been married. I tend to bet on two and six combinations, and I have yet to understand why people enjoy slot machines." She listened, fascinated, but she was returned to the present when he said, "Now that you know about me, why don't you tell me how I could have possibly destroyed your life."

She realized right then she would, but she had to figure out how to put it. She took a breath. "My husband…ex-husband is Travis Winston. Maybe you've heard the name?"

He shook his head. "Can't say that I have."

"Okay, I'm not surprised. He's just a small fish in your

world. He's not like you. He's not lucky, and he doesn't know when to stop gambling. If he has hunches, they're always wrong." Her hands were clenched now, her nails digging into her skin as she said a blunt truth. "He lost everything we had, and pretty much anything we ever would have at your place."

All he said was, "I'm not responsible for someone who can't control his gambling."

"Of course you aren't. That's what that man told me when I went there. 'We aren't the police or Gamblers Anonymous.' That's what he said. A night later, Travis was there and…" She bit her lip, the sting of tears behind her eyes infuriating. There was nothing to cry about anymore. Certainly not about Travis. Not about what would never be for Sierra.

She took a breath and words came out that shocked her with their hard truth. "You're just like Travis, except you're the flip side. You succeeded and he lost it all."

He didn't move, didn't even blink. "And I scare you, don't I?" he asked, his words jolting through her.

She glanced away, down at her hands, almost bloodless now from being clenched so furiously. He scared her. Yes, he did. On so many levels she couldn't sort them out.

"Holly?"

She heard him speaking but didn't look up. She concentrated on easing her hands open, pressing them flat against the fabric of her slacks on her thighs. Cain didn't speak again, didn't say a thing, until she finally gazed up at him. The impact of his words was nothing compared with the jolt at that moment, when she realized he'd leaned forward, much closer, and his eyes were holding hers. He terrified her, but not because of his nature, not because of what he did or didn't do. He terrified her because in that moment she felt a raw awareness of the man who rocked her world.

She could either get up and run, or stay and face him. She couldn't move—her legs wouldn't hold her. So she did the second thing. She stayed, and hoped that what she was experiencing would diminish. She was wrong again. As she sat there, neither of them speaking, that awareness just grew until she could barely think straight.

CAIN WATCHED HOLLY, part of him almost in pain from the tension he felt in her. He had his answer. Her husband had torn apart her life. She blamed Cain. He'd asked if he scared her, and he knew he did. He was a gambler. A man who lived by the cards. He stared down at his hands, then realized that he wasn't going to act as if nothing had been said by either of them. "Holly?" he asked as he looked back at her.

She took her time lifting her face to him, and he didn't miss the paleness in her skin. "I think I should get going now," she said in a rush.

He wanted to say, No way, or You're staying until I understand this, but all he said was, "Me, too," and stood.

He waited for her to stand. She did, clutching her purse as if it were her lifeline. And then he followed her back through the banquet room. All the festivities seemed oddly out of place now. She didn't stop walking until she got to the room where her daughter was being cared for. She would have gone inside if he hadn't halted her with a touch on her shoulder.

She jumped as if he'd burned her, and spun around to face him. There was color in her cheeks now, bright dots that warred with her hair. "Don't touch me," she muttered.

He drew back, his hand lifted, palm out toward her. "Sorry. I just thought we should finish what we started."

She shook her head, and a few strands of hair loosed themselves from the confines of the clips. One softly touched her cheek and he wanted nothing more than to brush the strands back for her. But he didn't. "We haven't started a thing, and never will."

He'd never begged a woman to listen to him, but he came damn close at that moment. "I told you about myself, as much as I could, and now I know about you. I thought it might help."

She bit her lip. "I appreciate what you said. It must have been a lonely time for you when you left here. And I don't blame you for what you are, or what you have to do."

That did it. "Well, thanks a whole damn lot for that," he muttered. "I wasn't lonely, by the way, and I do what I want to do—not what I have to do."

She flushed more deeply, and he regretted the harshness in his tone as soon as he'd uttered the words. "Of course," she whispered, turned from him and pushed back the door.

He watched the barrier close behind her, then headed for the private exit. He was out of there. Gone. Back to his world. A world she thought was lonely. A world that she thought had someway made her husband what he'd become. He grabbed the door, wrenched it open, and the cold hit him like a knife. He stood in the night, and for a split second, with the snow falling, obscuring all but the dim glow of the lights that defined the lifts on the mountain, he did feel lonely. He felt totally alone. He shook that off, and would have gone to his car if he hadn't spotted Malone coming toward him through the night.

"Got it all under control?" he asked the big man as he hurried up the stairs.

"Yeah, it's under control," Malone said, swiping at the snow clinging to his gray buzz cut. "How about the Winston woman? What's going on there?"

"She's getting her daughter. Dinner was canceled. Her sister and husband had to leave. She said to thank you, and she's going home."

"Oh, great," the man murmured. "Does she need a car?"

"I don't know," he answered.

"Look, I have to get up to the office. Can you find her and ask her about the car? If she wants one, call Raymond. But it'll be a bit of a wait. They're all in use for the next hour. After that, one will be available to take her home. Tell her to let the desk know where she'll be and they'll find her."

Cain didn't want to go back inside. He didn't want to see Holly again, but Malone was already grabbing the door and ducking inside. Cain went after him and caught up to him at the elevator. "Tell Jack I'll call him," he said as the big man got in the lift.

"Sure thing, sir," Malone said, then the door slid shut.

Cain hesitated. Just tell her about the damn car, he thought, or maybe leave her a note to explain. But before he could go find some stationery and a pen, the door to the play area opened and Holly was there. Louise was right beside her, carrying a bag. Holly had on a navy jacket and snow boots, and she was holding Sierra, who looked sound asleep in her mother's arms.

"I'm sure they can arrange something," Louise was saying, then saw Cain at the same time Holly did. "Oh, Mr. Stone. Hello. Have you seen Malone or—"

"He's up at the office," Cain said. "He asked me to make sure you had a car to go home in."

Louise was the one to appear relieved. "Oh, he took care of it," she said to Holly. "He's very efficient."

Holly rocked from side to side as she patted her daughter's back. "Okay, get the car," she said.

"Well, there's a problem. There won't be a car available for an hour or so."

"I can call a taxi," Holly said.

Cain shook his head. "There won't be a taxi available on a night like this."

That obviously wasn't what she wanted to hear. "I can't wait an hour."

"There's a lounge, and you could—" Louise was cut off.

"I can't wait." She looked at Cain. "Annie's sick. That's why they left. And Rick was going to come and get me, but he can't leave Annie. I can't just stay here."

Cain really was a betting man, but he knew that if he made a bet that he'd do the smart thing right then, he'd lose miserably. He moved closer to Holly. He took chances all his life, but when he spoke to Holly, he knew he was taking a huge chance. At least he was telling her the truth this time. "My car's outside. I'm on my way out of town, and I have to go right past the hotel."

Holly glanced at Louise, then back at Cain. "You don't have a car seat, and I don't—"

"I'll get one for you," Louise said. "We have some in storage. Just give me a couple of minutes."

She was gone, and Cain looked back at Holly. She didn't want to take a ride from him, he realized that, but she was plain out of options for how to get to her sister. "So, how about it?" he asked

"Okay, sure," she finally said.

"Stay here and I'll go warm up the car. I'm by the side entrance. When Louise gets back with the seat, have her come out with you."

He waited for her to nod in agreement, then he headed to the door. He went into the cold night, into the softly falling snow that had all but covered his car, and he got inside it. Once he started the motor and turned on the seat heaters, all he had to do was wait. It didn't take long for the side door to the Inn to open and Holly to come out, followed by Louise holding a car seat. Cain exited his vehicle and went around to open the passenger-side doors.

Louise fastened the safety seat on the backseat, then let Holly get closer. The SUV was high off the ground, and obviously, Holly couldn't step up with the child in her arms. "Here," he said, and got behind her, lifting both her and the child together so she could get her feet on the shaped running board and could duck into the car. She managed to get the child into the chair and fasten her in, Sierra barely stirring.

Holly half turned, grabbed the door edge and ignored the hand he held out to help her out. Instead, she jumped down herself. She pulled the door shut, then turned to Louise, who was getting covered with snow. "Thanks for everything," she said.

"You bet. We'll get together later on, okay?"

Holly nodded. "Sure, call me," she said, and turned to the front passenger door. She got inside the SUV, and Cain swung the door shut behind her. He thanked Louise, then went around and got in behind the wheel.

Cain put the car in gear and backed out, then headed slowly down the path toward the main gate. The night was getting worse, with a wind building and starting to drive the snow through the air.

"You're going back to Las Vegas tonight?" she asked, her voice soft in the interior of the car.

He glanced at her, and the glow from the dashboard lights defined shadows on her cheeks and at her eyes. "That was my plan," he murmured.

"The weather's horrible. It might not be a good idea to drive down the hill in it."

He wasn't looking forward to the drive, but he'd done it before in bad weather. Just head south and look for the lights in the sky from Las Vegas. "It's a miserable night," he admitted.

He sensed her turn toward him. "Why are you leaving?"

"Work."

"What about Christmas?"

"What about it?" he asked, watching as he hit some slow traffic when they got closer to the town itself.

"It's a holiday, in case you've forgotten."

"It's just another busy time for me."

"I'd think you'd celebrate making money," she said, and he wasn't sure if she was accusing him or trying to make a joke.

When he said, "It's all about money," he wasn't joking.

"Of course it is," she muttered, and her words made it sound as if he were admitting his job involved tearing the wings off butterflies.

"I'd guess you celebrate big-time?"

"Santa's very popular in our house."

He glanced in the rearview mirror at Sierra. "She'll learn."

"What's she supposed to learn?" she asked.

"That it's all a feel-good fairy tale that crashes and burns for most kids."

Shocked at his own cynicism, he expected her to attack him, or to scoff at him, or to reprimand him. She didn't do any of that. She simply said, "When did it end for you?"

Chapter Seven

Cain heard the question, and he didn't expect to know the answer to it. But he did. In a flash, he realized when the fantasy had ended for him. "I was seven." He slowed even more as the snow got heavier and the driving less easy. "I was always trying to believe in Santa, but for three years I'd asked for an harmonica, a silver one. My seventh year was the clincher. No harmonica. And I finally decided that Santa wasn't worth believing in."

He stared straight ahead, stunned that he'd told that. He wasn't a man given to sharing, not even when he was drunk. He was sober at the moment.

"So, you stopped believing," she murmured.

"Don't tell me you believe in Santa Claus?"

"Me? Oh, I have my suspicions about the old guy, but I'd never say them around Sierra."

He supposed that having kids changed a lot. He'd never find out if that was true or not. "What about Annie? What's wrong?"

"Rick didn't say, just that she was feeling really sick all of a sudden and he wanted to get her home. She's never sick—at least, not that I can remember."

He could hear the concern in her voice. "Everyone gets sick, sooner or later."

"I guess so," she said, then added, "There's the hotel. Go in the side lot."

The snow was already starting to obliterate the plowed parking lot, covering the cars with the white stuff. He pulled in as close as he could to the side entry of the tall building and stopped, leaving the car idling. "Why don't you go inside and check on Annie, see what's going on before you get Sierra out."

She looked taken aback, as if his thinking about the logic of leaving a sleeping child sleeping surprised her. "Okay," she said. "If you'll stay with her?"

"Of course," he said, and she got out.

He watched her through the windshield as the wipers slapped the heavy wet snow from side to side. She darted through the snow, ducking into the wind, then disappeared inside the hotel. He sank back on the seat. He had told her about Santa and him. He chuckled. That was something he hadn't told anyone, but when she'd asked, he'd spilled the beans. The woman affected him oddly. No, he thought, and chuckled again. It wasn't odd. She fascinated him. The child stirred and he glanced back at her. A cute child. He never noticed children. But she looked like her mother.

He heard a door slam and saw Holly running toward the car, going to the passenger door and pulling it open. She wasn't getting the child out but getting back in. She closed the door behind her, and as she sat back, brushing at her bright hair damp with clinging snow, she smiled at him with pure relief. "She's fine. She's sleeping."

He stared at her smile, and nothing else existed right then.

Not the storm outside or the sleeping child. Her smile stunned him. And that scared him more than anything had in his life, more than any chance he'd taken. "Great," he said, looking away from her to the snowy night as he put the car in gear.

HOLLY WAS GETTING READY to step into the shower, when she heard the sirens. The noise cut through the night, clearly heard over the growing storm outside. The sirens were coming closer, making the air in the small house almost vibrate with the noise. She put on her robe, then checked on Sierra to make sure she was still asleep, before heading for the front of the house.

Despite living on the street with the clinic, she'd never heard sirens like that. She went to the door to glance out and see what was going on, but when she pulled back the barrier, she almost ran into Cain on the front porch. She'd done nothing but think of him since he'd dropped her off, both what he'd told her and what she'd ended up telling him. As if those thoughts had materialized him, there he was, snow on his hair and the shoulders of his jacket, his car was parked where it had been fifteen minutes earlier, on the street.

He'd left quickly when he'd dropped her at the house, barely taking the time to help her inside with Sierra before he'd said goodbye. Now he was back, and the sound of sirens was everywhere. He said something to her that she couldn't hear, then she shouted to him, "What are you doing here?"

At the same instant she yelled, the sirens stopped and her voice echoed around them.

It made him grin for a moment, a really boyish expression of fun, and she had an idea of how he'd looked as a kid. Then she remembered what he'd said about Christmas and how he'd stopped believing. As his smile faded, her middle tightened.

"Sorry," she murmured, and shivered, suddenly aware that all she was wearing was her robe.

"Get inside," he said, motioning her back into the house. And when she did, he followed her, then shut the door behind them. He moved past her to the fire she'd built in the fireplace, holding his hands out to the heat from the flickering flames. She went closer, but kept the sofa between her and him. "What's going on?" she asked.

He rubbed his hands together, then turned to her. "Sorry to break in on you like this, but there was an accident."

"You were in an accident?" she asked, as she took in his damp hair, the flush in his face from the cold, searching for blood or scrapes…anything.

"No, not me. I saw Gordie on my way out, talked to him for a few minutes, then left. As I got to the end of the street, two cars hit head-on right in front of me."

"But you didn't get hit?" she asked.

"No," he said. "I missed the crash by seconds."

She wouldn't try to explain her overwhelming relief that he hadn't pulled out moments earlier and he wasn't hurt at all. "What…what about the others?"

"One guy's injured badly—cracked ribs, head wounds and a broken arm. Two others aren't in the best shape, either. I came back because the road was blocked with the cars and everyone trying to help." He exhaled with a bit of unsteadiness, and in that instant, he seemed almost…vulnerable. It was crazy to think of Cain Stone as vulnerable, but not as crazy as her wanting to help him when he shivered.

"You're freezing," she said, taking in the appearance of his damp coat and the way his hair clung to his temples. "Get out of your coat."

She watched him undo his coat, then slip it off his shoulders. That was when she moved closer, holding out her hand for the coat. He let her take it and she laid it on a chair beside the fireplace.

When she turned back to him, he was on his way to the couch. He sank down with a sigh, closed his eyes for a moment and stretched his legs out in front of him. He rested his hands on his thighs, then opened his eyes and looked up at her. Their blueness seemed shadowed in the firelight. Then they flicked over her, from her head to her bare feet and back again, meeting her gaze. "Sorry for intruding like this," he murmured.

She spoke in a rush. "No problem. How about some hot coffee?"

"That sounds good," he said as she headed into the kitchen.

She started a pot of coffee, then got mugs out of the cupboard by the door into the living room. To find Cain there, standing in the entrance, one shoulder against the jamb and his arms crossed on his chest, startled her. "You wouldn't have anything stronger to put in the coffee, would you?" he asked.

Right then a real drink sounded good to her, anything to settle nerves rapidly beginning to fray with Cain so close. "I'll check," she said, and waited for him to leave before she touched the counter and took a deep breath.

She found a bottle of cognac that she'd never opened, in the cupboard with the mugs, and when the coffee was done, she filled two mugs, put them on a tray and put the small bottle of cognac with them. When she went back into the living room, Cain was back on the couch, stretched out, staring at the fire. But when she got near, he looked up at her.

The irony of her position wasn't lost on her. Scant days ago, she'd thought she hated this man, that he was the reason so much was wrong in her life. Now the same man was sitting on her couch, making himself at home, silently opening the bottle of cognac and pouring a healthy dose of the alcohol in his coffee.

When she sat down on the couch, Cain held the bottle up to her. "Want some in your coffee?" he asked.

She wanted a long drink of it, but shook her head and reached for her mug of coffee. Drinking wouldn't be a good thing right then. She knew it, no matter how tempting it was at that moment. She cradled her mug on her lap, letting the heat from the china seep into her. Then she glanced to one side at Cain, and caught sight of his hands doing the same with his mug.

She realized how large his hands were, and that they weren't "fancy" hands at all. They weren't the hands of an indulgent man, as she'd thought they would be. His nails were square and unbuffed, and he had no gold rings on his strong fingers. The watch he wore was simple—a stainless-steel casing with a plain leather band. And there was a sprinkling of dark hair on his forearms. She saw him sit forward, his elbows resting on his knees, and he stared into the mug for a long moment before he took a drink of coffee. "Thanks for that."

She studied his profile, noting the tightness in his jaw and the way his eyes narrowed on the fire. She tasted her own coffee and let the heat slip down her throat. She turned to the fire, too, watching the way the flames licked the logs. Wind beat against the small house, driving snow at the windows and shaking the glass. She barely covered a shiver. "Anyone driving on a night like this is crazy," she murmured.

"I'm crazy?" Cain asked.

She met those blue eyes. "I meant, driving in this weather can be dangerous."

He rested his head against the cushions. "So I found out."

"So, you won't go to Vegas tonight?"

He drank more coffee, poured more cognac into the mug, then settled into the softness of the couch cushions. He stretched his legs out, finally put the mug on his stomach and didn't answer her question. "The coffee's good and the cognac is even better," he murmured.

"I'm glad you like it, but you haven't answered me. Are you going, or aren't you?"

He turned his head toward her. "If it clears."

"You can't," she said, sitting straighter.

He cocked one eyebrow at her. "I *can't?*"

"It just wouldn't be a good idea, not the sensible thing to do."

"Ah, spoken like a real teacher." He was grinning now, like a kid. "The old 'it's not a good idea to jump off that roof' speech, whose logic is irrefutable?"

"No, just common sense," she said, and glanced away from him, down into her own mug of coffee.

"Can I ask you something?" he asked.

She chanced a look at him again, and the smile was gone. "It depends."

"Why did you become a teacher?"

She shrugged. "I suppose I should say I wanted to help kids, but that's not it, not really. I've just always wanted to be a teacher. I never tried to figure out why. Oh, Travis used to say I liked to boss people, so being a teacher was natural."

"*Do* you like to boss people?"

"I don't think so, not usually. With Travis, I just had no choice. He said I treated him like a child, but..." She shrugged. "He sort of was. I felt I was taking care of two kids most of the time."

"What did he do for living?"

"At one time he was a draftsman. But he lost his job. Then we moved, and he worked in a warehouse. We moved again, and I thought he was working, then found out he was at the tables, trying to make a killing." She wondered why telling this man about Travis didn't bring the usual bitterness to her. Odd that it seemed to have morphed into a simple sadness. "He always talked big, always had a plan, but the last time the plan fell through, and I couldn't take it anymore."

She realized that Cain had shifted. His knee was now close to hers on the seat cushions. The drink rested on his thigh, and his eyes were on her. "It fell through at the Dream Catcher?" he asked in a low voice.

She stared into her now-tepid coffee. All she could do was nod. She didn't mention the locket Travis had pawned for his last spree, or the horrible day after their divorce had become final when she'd realized she and Sierra had to get as far from him as possible. When she knew she had to come back to Silver Creek.

Cain startled her by touching her chin with the tips of his fingers, gently lifting her face, but she kept her gaze down. "He lost more than money," Cain whispered. "What a fool."

That brought her eyes up to his, and the expression in them made her tremble. She turned her head, breaking the contact, and she remembered his comment about him scaring her. He did, and the fear almost choked her right then. Before she could get up and put distance between them, he touched her again. This time his hand cupped her chin and she didn't move. She could barely breathe.

He moved closer, so close she could feel his breath when he spoke. "A fool, a real fool," he said, and she knew exactly what was going to happen. The thing was, she didn't try to stop it. The kiss came gently. His lips brushing hers, his warmth on her, and she literally froze.

If she'd moved, she would have held on to him, she would have answered kiss for kiss, and the fear grew. His touch defined her world in a way she'd never experienced, and that touch was wrong. So wrong. She'd made so many mistakes, but her worst mistake had been letting her heart lead. Now her heart said to have more of this man, to know him more deeply, with an urgency that she hadn't ever felt with Travis. But her head told her to run like hell. To get out of there, to stop this soft exploration of his lips, then his hand, moving to her shoulder, around to her back, easing her toward him.

Help me, she thought, but couldn't fight. She couldn't stop the connection. *Help me,* echoed in her mind, but nothing in her would let her push back, let her break this off, let her do the smart thing. Then her pleas were answered by a banging on the front door and a voice calling, "Cain? Cain? Are you in there?"

The sound of his name drew Cain out of a parallel universe, a universe where he had come to Holly's house, even though he could have simply stayed in his idling car until the mess at the end of the street had been cleared. It had been his choice to return. Pure and simple. He'd sat with her in front of the fire, knowing her daughter was in the next room, and he'd reached out for her on impulse and kissed her. He'd jumped in feet first and hadn't looked back. Taking a chance was one thing, but this time he'd put more than money on the line with his gamble.

The moment his lips had touched hers, he'd known he'd

wanted to do that since his first glimpse of her stepping off Jack's elevator. He'd wanted to, and now he had. But if he'd thought one kiss would shock him into sanity, he'd been sadly mistaken. It only pulled him further into that insanity. He drew back, and then he was looking down at her, into eyes that echoed his own stunning shock at what had just happened.

"Cain!" The voice was there again, along with more pounding.

Gordie. Cain didn't say a thing to Holly. Truth be told, he didn't know what to say, so he stroked her silky cheek, and felt her tremble. For an instant he thought, To hell with Gordie. But he made himself draw back even more, then stand and turn from her to go to the door. At the same moment Gordie called out "Cain!" again, the child started to cry from another part of the house.

Cain went to the door, aware of Holly going the opposite way, to her child, and that brought everything into perspective. They were going in opposite directions in every sense of the word. He opened the door to find Gordie standing there, hand raised to knock again. He was bundled in heavy clothes, and a fur hat, with snow clinging to it, was pulled low over his head. Snow still fell behind him, but a softer version than had been the case an hour ago. "The road's cleared," he said, and eyed the fire blazing in the hearth. "Glad you found some heat in here."

At any other time, Cain would have laughed at Gordie's unintentional double entendre. "Yeah, I did," he said, not feeling much like laughing then.

Gordie smiled at the room behind him. "Holly, hello."

She was there, near Cain, but not beside him. She hung back a bit. "Is everything okay now?" she asked.

"Everyone's damn lucky," Gordie said. "Including Cain. A moment earlier and he would have been in the middle of the mess." He grinned at Cain. "He's always been a lucky son-of-a—" He cut off his words and ended with, "His luck's holding." He shifted his attention to Cain. "If you're going, you'd better get going down while the plows are keeping the roads passable."

Cain realized he had been thinking about heading back to the Inn for the night—at least, until he heard Sierra start to complain behind him. He'd told Holly he followed his hunches, and right then, despite the fact he knew he wanted more with the mother, his hunch was it was a bad idea. It was a bad gamble. "Thanks."

"Sure. You'll be back for the wedding?"

"I wouldn't miss it," he said, then Gordie said good-night to Holly and walked out into the snowy night.

Cain turned and Holly was right there with Sierra in her arms. The child was cuddling in, one arm around her mother's neck, and all Cain could think of was Holly's taste, which must still be on his lips. Wordlessly, he went around her, grabbed his coat, warmed from the fire, and shrugged into it. When he turned around she was by the sofa, the child obviously back to sleep in her arms.

"Thanks for everything," he said.

She closed her eyes for a moment, then met his gaze again. "You drive carefully," was all she said.

"That's the plan."

He headed for the door, but as he got abreast of Holly, he found himself stopping. Her face tilted up to his, her lips parted softly, and he knew it wasn't an invitation for anything more. But he ignored that bit of sanity, and bent to brush her forehead with his lips, then he left.

He stepped out into the cold, and as he made his way through the snowdrifts to his car by the curb, he felt an emptiness in him that bordered on painful. He hunched into the cold, went around and got into his car, starting it quickly to get the heater going. But he didn't drive away immediately. He sat there on the pretext of warming up the interior, watching his windshield wipers slap back and forth against the falling snow.

"Go back," he told himself. "Go home." But in that moment, he realized he didn't have a home. He had a place he stayed, a place he worked. But no home. And he glanced at Holly's house through the drifting snow, and observed the soft light spilling out of the living-room window. He saw a flash of movement behind the sheer drapes, then it was gone. He put his car in gear and drove away.

THE NEXT MORNING at dawn, Cain didn't wake up in his penthouse on the top floor of the Dream Catcher Hotel. He woke up in the luxury cottage at the Inn. He'd driven to the edge of town, and when he'd seen the plow ahead of him, trying to push the snow away as fast as it fell, he'd pulled over to the side of the road. This was crazy. He was driving when he shouldn't be. Surely the accident earlier underscored how dangerous driving was that night.

He'd sat there for a while, then finally made a U-turn and headed back toward the Inn. Jack had been as good as his word, keeping the cottage open for him, and he'd taken him up on it for at least one more night.

He stretched out in the large bed and stared up at the ceiling. It was barely dawn, and he was wide awake. He'd spent a restless night, with odd dreams that he wasn't going to try to recapture. Holly had been in them, but the old orphanage had been there, too, the school, the mountain, his past, and they hadn't made sense.

He sat up and went naked into the bathroom to the shower. He let the warm water wash over him, but when the thoughts of Holly last night, the kiss that he'd allowed to happen, came back to him, he stepped out and grabbed a towel. His body didn't have the sense to know when to respond to memories and when not to, and he wasn't going to let himself ache for something that would never be and never should be.

He went back into the bedroom, then saw the skiing equipment he'd used before, all neatly arranged on top of a huge trunk against the wall. Why not? Maybe he could think in the fresh air. Half an hour later when he left the cottage, he had no intention of going up the mountain. He'd thought he was just heading to the high lift on the resort land. But when he got there, he'd ended up going over the back fence and trudging toward Killer Run.

At the top, he pushed his poles into the snow and surveyed his surroundings. The bitter cold would have cut through any clothes, except the specially manufactured skiing outfit he had on. Clouds hung heavy in the sky, and he doubted the sun would make any appearance all day. The chill wouldn't ease at all. He found himself searching for a flash of yellow in the snow-laden trees, but there was none. He wasn't sure if he was relieved or disappointed when he tossed his skis onto the snow and went about buckling them onto his boots with the bindings.

Finally, he stood, then turned to the valley far below. The familiarity of the snowy scene touched something in him, and for a fleeting moment, he almost felt he was looking at home. He shook his head, pulled his goggles down and went to the edge of the jump. Home? Not even close. He had no home. He'd never had; he never would.

He dug his poles into the snow, crouched and pushed off. He started out straight, but one of his skis caught, and suddenly, he was in the air, but going sideways when he should have been going straight. And he was lost. His poles were gone and his hands flailed, but there was nothing to catch to stop his fall. The scream he heard was his own, echoing back at him as he plunged downward.

He figured he'd be okay as long as he went directly down, but when he realized he was angling away from the run, he knew he was going toward real danger. The mountain was rugged, with rock ledges over steep drops, all hidden by snow. And he was heading into territory where even a few feet of snow wouldn't cushion him. He tried to twist, tried to get his hands out to break the impact, but nothing worked.

When the impact came, it was hard, and cold, and painful. There was a moment when snow was everywhere, like the pain that engulfed his body, then he lost consciousness. Blackness enveloped him, and he was gone. Then out of the blackness he heard a sound. It came from a far-off, almost ethereal place, drifting around him and echoing through him. It was his name, said over and over again.

As it drew him out of unconsciousness, it became more real, more intense. He worked to take a deep breath, then felt the blackness fade, and he knew he was alive. He was on his back, pain radiating up his side, to his shoulder and into his head. And that voice was there.

"Cain? Cain! Can you hear me?"

He wanted to say he could, that he heard the voice clearly,

but when he tried to open his eyes and respond, he found it harder to do than he'd expected. He had to concentrate to make his eyes open to the grayness of blurred land and sky.

"Cain! Oh, God, answer me!" the voice demanded.

Then he saw color, a small dot of it, brilliant in the grayness, and as his eyes focused, he realized the color was Holly's hair. Holly. Either he was hallucinating, or she was above him, yelling down at him. He tried to lift his hand, but it fell weakly onto his stomach.

"Cain! I'm here. I'm here," she shouted to him.

Blackness threatened to overtake him again. He fought it. He lay very still, gazing a good thirty feet to Holly. He must have landed on a ledge, at a spot where the cliff face looked as though it shot straight up.

He groaned as he attempted to sit up, and he heard Holly yell to him. "Oh, my God, be careful."

He shoved himself to a sitting position, and as his head cleared, he knew he wasn't hurt badly. The snow must have cushioned a lot of the impact after all. He had pain in his head and one shoulder, but his legs were okay. He could move them. He pushed away from the drop-off, toward the rock wall, and managed to get to his feet. He stood very still. Holly was talking to him from above, but her voice swam around him. He couldn't focus on it. All he could do was press his hand on the wall and keep his balance.

"Stay still and I'll get help," he finally understood she was saying.

Without glancing up, afraid he'd fall backward, he tried to call to her, but his voice was little more than a croak. Then he coughed and tried again. This time he could speak. "No, I…I'm okay. Just find some rope."

"No, you can't—" she started to tell him.

He cut her off, risking a glance up at her. And he didn't fall backward after all. He was standing on his own two feet and he wasn't falling. "Get rope, long enough to reach, heavy enough for my weight."

She hesitated, and he said, "Get rope," and sank back into the snow.

"Okay, okay," she shouted. "Just…don't move."

He nodded, burying his face in his hands, and when he finally looked back up to the top, she was gone. He saw blood on his gloves, and he waited for her to return.

He felt the snow fall on him first, then heard Holly saying, "I'm here," and he saw a dark cord dangling over the side, toward him. "I tied it onto the big tree."

He made himself stand again, the effort less intense this time, and when the rope reached where he was, he stretched to grab it with the blood-spotted gloved hand. The rope was thick and new, and he tilted his head back to look up.

She was there, and no way could he explain the rightness he felt at seeing her looking down at him, except to believe that it was because she came to rescue him. She'd been there when he needed her, and she was the only one who could get him back to the top. The only one. He shoved all that aside.

"Good work," he called. Then, with both hands coiling the rope tightly in his grasp, he started the painful trip up to Holly.

Chapter Eight

Holly could barely breathe as she watched Cain climb toward her through the snow, rappelling awkwardly off the side of the drop, hand over hand, upward. She felt her hands clench in her gloves, and it was all she could do not to keep from stretching down to try to help. What if she hadn't come today, if she had gone with Annie and Sierra to get a Christmas tree, if she hadn't decided that today was the day to go back to the cabin? Who would have found Cain?

She saw him slowly make his way higher, awkwardly go hand over hand, closer and closer, then she reached out to him. She grabbed at his glove, felt it start to slip, and she quickly caught at his wrist, exposed where the cuff of his jacket had slipped back. She clasped his wrist and pulled with all her might.

Cain was there in a rush, tumbling forward into the snow, shoving her back with him and ending up half on top of her, his weight taking away her breath. His face was inches from hers, and she felt his rapid breathing, warm on her face. She saw the blood on his head, but his eyes were clear and he was alive. He moved off her, pushing himself awkwardly to his feet, then he was the one holding out a hand, helping her get up.

She let him capture her hand with his and held tightly as he lifted her to her feet, then she was facing him. She had to tilt her head back to look into his eyes, and remembered his telling her when Santa had died for him. A belief in something. Gone. Right then she wished she'd been there, that she'd been able to get him what he'd needed, and kept that belief alive, even if only for another year.

Crazy thought, she told herself, and made herself speak rationally. "You've cut your head," she said, squinting at the wound to blur out the man's features. "You might require stitches." He shivered, and she realized snow was clinging to him everywhere, even his hair. His goggles were around his neck, snow dug into the collar of his jacket and his skis were nowhere in sight. "We have to get you to the doctor's."

"I'll be fine," he said through clenched teeth, and she knew that was a lie. He was freezing and probably in shock. But she didn't argue with him. She took his arm, and knew how "unfine" he was when he leaned toward her. She kept her hold on him and started trudging back the way she'd come, blotting out the memory of the scream that had echoed through the trees and drawn her to the jump.

Cain's stride got stronger as they went, and by the time the cabin was in view, he was drawing back from her, breaking the connection. She let him go ahead of her, watching him trudge in her old footsteps in the newly fallen snow, heading for the cabin. She stared at his back, then glanced past him at the house. In the gray light it appeared dreary, small and all but covered with snow. The only welcoming sign was the smoke from the fire she'd laid earlier.

She hurried around Cain, up the steps on the porch, and quickly opened the door to let him inside. The heat from the glowing fire almost hurt her face. She tugged off her jacket, tossed it onto a nearby chair in the single-room cabin and looked at Cain. He was swinging the door shut behind him. Then he started to undo the fasteners on his jacket.

His fingers fumbled with the top snap. With a low oath, he grabbed the jacket on either side and tugged. The snaps all gave way. Holly helped him tug the wet jacket off. She pulled to get his arms free, then put the jacket on a chair by the one that held hers. "I don't have a phone here to call a doctor," she said as she watched him walk slowly to the sofa, a well-worn plaid thing that sagged in the middle. "And my cell works if it's clear and bright and it decides to work. I'll try it and see if—"

"I don't need a doctor. I just need to get warm," he said, sitting forward and holding his hands out to the fire's heat.

The blood from the cut was drying, making the jagged line just above his left eye even uglier. She went into the kitchen, which consisted of little more than a couple of cupboards, a tiny wood stove and a refrigerator by the sink, got a first-aid kit and went back to the sofa. She sat by Cain, put the first-aid box on the rough wooden table in front of them and opened it.

She took out a packet, tore it open to get to a pad soaked in an antiseptic solution. She reached for Cain with her free hand, her fingertips touching his chin, feeling the bristle from the start of a new beard. She eased his face toward her, and wasn't prepared for the impact of his blue eyes as they met hers. "This will clean it up," she said quickly, and concentrated on wiping the dead blood away from the wound. In reality, the wound was about an inch long, more a tear than a cut. And as soon as she'd cleared the clotted blood, the wound started to bleed again.

She pressed the pad to it, then said, "Hold this."

He lifted his hand, touching hers; then his fingers found the pad and pressed it to his forehead. She got a bandage, opened it, then turned back to Cain. "Okay, take that off," she said, and as soon as he lowered the pad, she put the bandage over the cut and secured it. "There," she murmured as she sat back, studying her work. "It's crooked, but the cut's not bleeding through it. I really think you need a stitch or two."

He held out the bloody pad to her. "I'm a fast healer."

And, just the way Gordie had said the night before, he was lucky. The way he'd fallen, he could have struck his head more severely, and if she hadn't heard him… She didn't complete that thought. Not when it made her start to shake. She took the pad, pushed it in a disposal bag along with the wrappings from the bandage. "We'd better get going," she said, standing to put the first-aid kit back in the kitchen. But Cain stopped her with his words.

"This place hasn't changed, has it?"

She looked down at him. "How would you know if it changed or not? You've never been in here."

He sat back, letting his head rest against the back of the couch and glanced up at her from under lowered lashes. "You sound so sure of yourself."

She sat down again, her mission forgotten for the moment. "You were never in here," she repeated.

"Very sure of yourself," he said softly, and she could have sworn he was about to smile.

She tossed the first-aid kit onto the table. "What are you talking about?"

"I was in here."

She frowned at him. "When?"

"Let me think," he murmured. "I'm thirty-eight now, and I was fourteen then, so twenty-four years ago and it still looks the same."

"No way."

"Way."

"My father let you in?"

"I didn't say that, did I?"

"You broke in?"

"Well, I didn't say that, either. Actually, I *came* in. The door was unlocked and I was cold and tired, and I had to walk all the way back to town. I'd cracked one of my skis. If it happened now, I'd just pretend I was snowboarding and head down, but then, you didn't do that. No one was here, so I came in, lit a fire, stayed awhile, then left."

"That's…that's breaking and entering," she said, and knew how stupid that sounded.

"One of my lesser crimes," he murmured.

She sank onto the sofa, and stared at the fire. She had no idea he'd ever been here.

She must have frowned, because Cain said, "Hey, I'm not a serial killer."

She should laugh, make a joke out of it, but there was no humor in her at that moment. There was just Cain, so close she felt his body heat. Cain, who had invaded her life even when she hadn't realized he had. Cain, who was making her so damn aware of the way his hair curled damply at his temples and the way the light exposed the hollow at his throat. Cain.

"I know you think I'm scum," he said, so wrong that she almost laughed right then. "I'm a gambler and a risk taker. Hell, it was a risk coming in here when your dad would have shot me if he'd found me." Then she looked at him, and he smiled at her, a sudden, devastating expression. "But he didn't. My luck held, even then."

The urge to touch him was there so abruptly and so strongly that she almost lost her breath. "You and your damn luck," she muttered, and moved, hitting him in the shoulder in the process and sending him back into the sofa. "Ouch," he gasped, and she saw him grimace and clutch his shoulder.

"You're hurt," she said, and reached for him. He grimaced again when she touched his shoulder through his shirt, and she thought he was a bit paler now. "Maybe you broke your shoulder."

He drew back, stood, then tugged his shirt out of his pants and unbuttoned it. He started to take it off, but gasped when he tried to pull his arm out of the sleeve. Holly stood and reached for the soft cotton thermal, then eased it off his shoulders. She flinched at the bruise on the cap of his right shoulder, oddly round, about eight inches across, in yellow, purple, green and blue.

"Oh, my gosh," she whispered.

He flexed his shoulder carefully, then lifted his hand, balled his fingers into a fist, then exhaled. "It's not broken."

"How can you tell?" she asked, swallowing hard.

He eased back down, leaving his shirt half off and exposing a strong chest with just an arrow of dark hair that disappeared into his pants. "I've had enough broken bones," he said.

She sat with him. "Well, you're not a doctor and that looks ugly. You need to get it taken care of."

"You really are bossy, aren't you?" he said with the shadow of a smile.

But she wasn't amused. His comment hit a nerve in her. Travis had told her that so often and she'd told Cain about it.

"You're bossy. You're trying to run my life," Travis had yelled at her, and she'd been so used to it, that the words rolled right off her back after a while. But coming from Cain, the remark hurt. "Whatever," she muttered, and started to get up. However, Cain stopped her.

He caught her hand with his, holding her so she couldn't get out of there, and when she attempted to jerk free, his hold on her tightened. She glanced down at him. "Let me go."

"What just happened?" he asked, ignoring her order.

She looked up at the ceiling, but was totally aware of the strength of his hand touching her despite his hurt shoulder. "Nothing."

He tugged her down onto the sofa with a tug on her hand, his eyes were on hers, not blinking. "I was kidding, and you're probably right. I should let Gordie take a look at me."

She went limp, and bit her lip hard. She could feel the sting of tears behind her eyes and she cursed the way she responded to Cain, even when he was trying to kid with her. Had Travis ruined even that for her? That a man could be attempting to have fun, and she felt nothing but pain? Or that she could look at a man, a man she could want, and she felt this overriding sense of it being so wrong?

"Hey, I don't say I'm sorry too often, but I'm sorry," Cain murmured, then unexpectedly brushed at her hair by her temples. "I'm really sorry."

"It…it isn't you," she managed in a choked voice. But it *was* him. "It's…it's just…"

"Hey," he said, and gently gathered her into his chest.

And she let him. She went into his heat and comfort, and held to him. The tears didn't come, but something in her settled, and a pain she hadn't been aware of started to dissolve.

She pressed her face into his bare chest, heard his heart beating and felt so centered it stunned her.

"It's okay," Cain whispered against her hair. "It's okay."

And it was, it really was, until she realized how very unokay it was for her to hold on to this man, to feel what she was feeling and to want it never to end. She made herself push back, and he didn't stop her. She made herself take a breath to ease a growing tension in her, and she almost got herself to stand and walk away.

If Cain hadn't touched her again, if he hadn't put one finger to her lips, if she hadn't felt a vague unsteadiness in the man, she would have broken the contact. But she didn't. She couldn't.

Cain knew right then that he wanted Holly as much as he'd ever wanted a woman. No, it felt like more, much more, and despite the fact that they hadn't had much time together, he felt something in him that he'd never felt before. A real need for someone else. That was something he'd never allowed himself to feel. Ever. Until now. The idea had always been unthinkable. Until now.

He smoothed her full bottom lip with the tip of his finger, then moved closer, needing to taste what his finger touched. And as he found her lips with his, as he felt the soft warmth under his, as they opened to him, he recognized how much of a risk taker he was. He realized how dangerous it was to let this grow, to allow himself to feel what he was experiencing, but he didn't turn from it. He didn't turn from her.

He was there, in every sense of the word, a man full of longing that he hadn't even known was in him. He groaned and drew her into him, and she was so close that he felt her heart beating against his. He felt the swell of her breasts on his chest, and the scent of her permeated him, filtering into his being, down to his soul.

He shifted, pulling her into his lap, feeling her legs go around his hips, her arms around his neck; her taste was everywhere. He kissed her jaw, the sweep of her throat when she arched back. Then he found the buttons on her shirt and slowly undid them, one by one, experiencing the silky heat of her skin under his touch. The cotton of her shirt was gone, and his hand felt lace, then skin again, her breast in his hold, the hardening of her nipple.

His whole body responded, a rush of desire burned through him, and he turned, falling back into the sofa with her under him, her lips on his skin, her hands finding his stomach, then the waistband of his pants. Her fingers were under the constriction, pushing lower. The snap gave way, and her hand was on him, with only the thin cotton of his Jockey shorts between him and her touch. He groaned at the contact, trembling from the feelings that coursed through him, and he dipped his head, catching her nipple in his mouth.

She arched into him, her hand tightening on him, and he knew he was getting to the point where nothing could make him stop. He drew back enough to look down at her under him, to look into sensation-glazed eyes a deep, vibrant amber. He wanted her. Plain and simple. No, there was nothing plain and simple about what he felt for this woman. Nothing. "Are you sure?" he made himself ask. He hated the whole idea of stopping. Then he hated himself as her eyes focused on him.

Her hands stilled; then, with agonizing slowness, she drew back from him. She turned her face into the pillows of the couch, and her voice was unsteady and vaguely muffled, "No, I…I can't. I…I…can't."

His body ached, but he rolled off her and got to his feet. He couldn't hide the desire that still stayed in his body. He didn't try to, even when she sat up. Her head was bent as she pulled her bra back down over her small, high breasts, covering the rosy nipples, hiding the alabaster skin. Then she was tugging her shirt closed, ignoring the buttons.

He didn't know what to say, so he said nothing. He turned from her, pulled at his own shirt, ignoring the flaring pain in his shoulder, then did up the waistband of his pants and left his shirt out. He couldn't stop the shuddering sigh as he crossed to get his jacket. It was warm from the fire but still damp. He didn't care. He put it on quickly. His taking a risk was one thing. She wasn't about to take any risk, not with him.

When he finally turned back, his body had stopped responding to what hadn't happened, but he hadn't. He saw Holly moving to put the first-aid tin in the cupboard, then she came toward him but went past him to the fireplace. She prodded at the fire with a poker, banking it, then put away the poker. That was when she made a grab for her coat right by him.

He couldn't handle things any longer. He grabbed her coat at the same time, not letting go when she tried to free it. She finally looked up at him, her eyes overly bright, her face pale. "What?" she breathed.

"You tell me. What?"

She held tightly to her coat, never letting go. "Just give it to me," she said, looking down at the piece of material stretched between them and not up at him any longer.

He let go suddenly, taking no pleasure in the way she swayed backward for a moment from the quick release. She put the coat on, missing the sleeve with her hand twice before she finally made it work. He didn't help for the simple reason that if he touched her again, he wasn't quite sure what he'd do. So he waited. But if he thought she'd say something then, he was wrong…again.

She moved away from him to the door. She stopped to put on her boots, then she opened the door. That was when she turned to him, but her eyes didn't meet his. "Are you coming?"

He went to the door, took his time putting on his boots, then followed her out into the biting cold of day that had grown even grayer. He stared at her hard as she led the way to her car, the small blue compact now almost hidden by the snow. She swiped at the windshield with a gloved hand, then opened the door and got inside. He went around and got in the passenger side in time to see the windshield wipers start to strain at the snow, before finally pushing the snow aside so he could see out the window.

The silence was deafening on the way home, and their progress was painfully slow. The snow was letting up some, but the roads were slippery and there was no clearing on the higher roads. The plows hadn't made it past the Inn, and by the time Holly pulled up to the security check at the front gates, Cain was ready to get out and walk the rest of the way.

The guard looked at the small car, frowned, then headed over to it. He didn't smile even when he saw Cain. The frown deepened at the sight of the head wound and he leaned in closer. "You okay, Mr. Stone?"

"Yeah, just fine," he murmured.

The guard glanced at Holly, then opened the gates for them. Holly drove toward the main lodge, and when they got close to the side entrance, Cain finally spoke. "My cabin's back there," he said.

For a minute he thought she was going to ignore him completely and dump him at the side entrance, and she probably should have. But she swung to the left, onto the cleared route, and headed into the compound. "Which one?" she asked.

"The last cabin."

She drove in silence, keeping her speed to a crawl, and at last pulled up in front of his unit. She spoke again as she looked out at the building. "This is a cabin?"

He glanced at the structure. It was double storied, as big as a small house, with a steeply pitched roof, wide stone steps going up to a heavily carved door with inset stained glass, under a wide roof supported by sturdy peeled log posts. "That's what they call it around here," he said.

"Yeah," she breathed, and finally looked at him. "Can you get inside yourself?"

"I've been walking since I was..." He shrugged. "Actually, I don't know how old I was when I walked. They didn't keep those records at the orphanage."

He thought he saw her grimace before she turned away from him. He grabbed the latch, opened the door and got out, shocked that his head felt light for a moment and he had to grip the door frame till he got his focus back. That was when he realized she was right by him. She must have gotten out, but he hadn't been aware of it until her hand grabbed his arm and she said, "Take it easy."

He looked down at her, his body with a life of its own, responding to the sight of her upturned face, the lips that he knew the taste of and the eyes that had, for a moment in time, been as filled with as much need as his own.

He released the door, perfectly stable at the moment, but he allowed her to walk with him up the steps, onto the entry porch. He took his key card out of his pocket, but his hand was less then steady for some reason, and she finally took the card from him when he couldn't get it aligned with the slot. She put it in, the door clicked, and she went with him into the cabin.

The minute they were inside, she let go of him and he didn't miss the low whistle as she looked around. "Good heavens!" she said as he watched her eyes flick from luxury to luxury. "What does Jack get a day for this place?"

He shrugged. "I don't have any idea," he said truthfully. He'd never thought about it before.

She shoved her hands into the pockets of her jacket. "If you're okay...?" she said to him.

"I'm fine," he said—an absolute lie. He could barely think of anything but what had almost happened, and damn it, his body hadn't forgotten a moment of it. He bent down carefully, undoing the buckles on his boots, then stood to step out of them, balancing himself with one hand on the wall to his left. He pushed the boots to one side and started to removed his jacket as he glanced back at Holly.

As soon as their eyes met, Holly stammered, "Well, if—if you're okay, I—I'll—"

"You'll what?"

He realized she was uncomfortable, and on some level, he enjoyed it. God knows he was uncomfortable enough himself at that moment. He heard her take an unsteady breath, and there was a flash of that look he'd seen at the first, a look that was almost painful for him at that moment. "I'll leave."

"Sure you will," he said. "Thanks for rescuing me, although you probably wish I'd gone all the way down and disappeared forever."

Color flooded her face, rivaling her hair for brilliance, and her eyes got overly bright and large. "Oh, no…I never wished that."

He felt immediate contrition, a new experience for him. Usually, he said what he thought and didn't give a damn how the person received it. At the moment, he did give a damn. "You've got a right to feel any way you want to about me."

That brought even more pain in her expression. "Oh, damn it," she muttered, and turned from him, reaching for the door.

He couldn't allow her to go. Not like this. If he was frustrated and angry, so be it. That was his problem. He wasn't out to hurt her at all. Period. He moved with her, caught her by the arm and stopped her. He drew back when she pulled free of his hold. "Hey, let's start again? I'm in a foul mood, and I don't have any reason to think that you…that any of this is what you wanted. I'll apologize for what happened, or didn't happen, in the cabin."

She was very still, nibbling on her bottom lip nervously. She was barely two feet from him and he could see a pulse racing in her throat where the top button of her jacket was open. "Boy," she whispered, "I don't do this well at all."

Those eyes met his, and now there was confusion in them. "You don't do what?" he asked, refraining from touching her, no matter how enticing the idea of contact with her was. "Do what?" he asked.

She shook her head. "Listen, what happened, I…I didn't mean to…"

He did let himself touch her then, let himself cup her chin and feel the unsteadiness in her. He eased her head up, until her eyes met his. "Holly, you listen to me. I meant it up there, if you weren't sure, that's it." Damn, he sounded noble, but he was saying the truth. He'd never forced a woman to do anything, and he sure as hell wouldn't force

Holly Winston to do anything she didn't want as much as he did. "It's too fast. Too much." And he wanted it so much his body ached.

Her tongue touched her lips, and the action ran riot over his raw nerves. "No, it's just wrong," she said in a voice so low he could barely hear it.

"Wrong?"

She shook her head. "Wrong. It's crazy, and it shouldn't have happened, and it won't happen again."

As she said the words, he felt a gut reaction to them. Pain. Pure and simple. Pain. He'd never known that before, an emotional wrenching in him. But before he could figure it out, he realized that he was starting to slip, that his head was light and his legs were losing their strength. He heard Holly say his name, and he reached out for the back of the couch. The leather was under his hand, solid support, and he took a deep breath.

He thought he was okay. But the next instant, Holly had him by the arm and was pulling him around the back of the couch. She eased him onto the couch, into the softness of the leather cushions. "You either go to the clinic, or I'll call the doctor," she said firmly, standing over him.

He would have argued; he would have told her that neither thing was going to happen. But right then, the world got unsteady again. He shook his head, closed his eyes and said, "I'm not going anywhere."

He was startled when her hand brushed his forehead coolly. The contact jolted him, and he looked back up at her. "Okay, fine by me," she said, then reached for the phone. When she put in a call for the in-house doctor, he gave up.

For some reason, the idea of her taking care of him was appealing. He knew why. No one had ever done that for him.

No one had just made all the decisions and taken care of him. Usually, he hated losing control. But right then, he just settled back and let her do it.

Chapter Nine

The doctor got there in ten minutes, bag in hand, fur hat covering his head, and she was shocked he was Doc Gordie. She'd expected a house doctor from the lodge, and even if they'd called Gordie at the clinic, it took at least fifteen minutes to get to the Inn. As though he read her surprise at his appearing so quickly, he explained as he came inside. "I was taking care of a gimpy skier at the main lodge, and they told me Cain was hurt," he said, and put his black bag on the nearest chair, then removed his hat and coat.

She motioned to Cain, who hadn't budged from the couch. "He fell off the run at the top of my property and hit his head. I put a bandage on it, but I…" She followed Gordie as he headed for the couch with his bag.

"What a surprise. I thought you'd left last night for the city," Gordie said as he opened his bag on the coffee table.

"That was the plan," Cain murmured.

"Instead you went skiing on the Killer?"

Gordie started to peel off the bandage to check the wound, and Cain grimaced. "I was going to, but I tripped."

"Ah, the old 'I tripped' routine, huh?" he asked as he exposed the raw wound and started to clean it.

"Skis tangled, Gordie," Cain murmured.

"Sure, they did," the doctor said. "Looks like you need a stitch or two."

"Forget it. Just slap something on it so I won't bleed all over the place."

Gordie took out a butterfly bandage, then smoothed it on the gash and glanced up at Holly. "So, you doctored him up when he did this?"

She nodded. "I tried."

"She got me off a ledge," Cain said. "Damn well saved my life."

Gordie smiled at her. "You saved his life?"

She was standing by the couch, concentrating on what he was doing to Cain. "I heard him scream and found him. He wouldn't go to the clinic or anything."

"I bet he wouldn't," Gordie said as he finished with the bandage. "And if he won't have stitches, we'll just pull it together and hope for an interesting scar." He sat back, looking at Cain, who was studying his hands, which were resting on his thighs. "I can't say you'll be dashing, but the scar shouldn't be too horrible."

Cain shrugged and Holly saw him wince. "He's got a terrible bruise on his right shoulder," she said.

Cain moved then, glancing up at her with a frown. "It's just a bruise."

Gordie didn't ask permission as he started to undo Cain's shirt, then pulled it back. The bruise was uglier now, on the cap of his shoulder and down his arm about ten inches. He spoke to Cain, asking him to wiggle his arm and his fingers, then he sat back and reached for his bag. He took out a small bottle. "It doesn't appear broken, and I know you won't go in for X-rays, so use a couple of these for the pain, and if it you have any numbness in your hand, get in touch with your doctor in Vegas."

"Sure," Cain agreed as he awkwardly tugged his shirt back on but left it undone.

Holly didn't glance at the sleek expanse of his exposed chest. She remembered too vividly how it had felt to touch him. She pushed her hands behind her back while the doctor closed up his bag and stood. He gave her instructions as if she was Cain's nurse. "Don't let him sleep for at least two hours. If he starts to get dizzy, if he throws up or he gets a bad headache, call me. If he passes out, dial 911 immediately."

"Oh, I'm not staying," she said quickly—too quickly. Both men frowned at her.

"Okay," Gordie said, elongating the single word the way some people would a whistle. "I guess I'll get Jack to send someone down to stay with him, but he shouldn't be alone at all."

She wanted out of there, away from the man with the open shirt and the look in his eyes that made her legs weak and robbed her of all sanity. But short of saying "Too bad" and leaving right then, she believed she didn't have a choice. "I guess I could stay for a bit," she said, adding in a rush, "at least until someone comes."

"Good, good," Gordie said, snapping his bag shut.

Cain and Gordie spoke for a few minutes, then Gordie was gone, and Holly was left knowing this was wrong, dead wrong. But nothing would happen, she told herself, averting her eyes from Cain. She wouldn't let it. Her decisions with men had been nothing but bad since she'd met Travis; she didn't trust her reactions anymore. And she certainly had a reaction to Cain. Her anger hadn't been over Cain being a bad person; he wasn't. But she realized how devastatingly attractive he was to her and had been from the beginning. What had happened at the cabin had been inevitable, but now it was over. It was done, and when she left, she wouldn't be back.

She closed the door after Gordie left, then turned and saw Cain hadn't moved. He was lying on the sofa, his eyes closed. "You can't go to sleep," she said.

She thought he murmured "I know," but he didn't open his eyes.

"How about some coffee?" she asked, going to the sofa.

"Sure," he said softly, his eyes still closed.

"You have to sit up and open your eyes," she said.

He finally stirred, pushing himself up, and his eyes opened. He glanced up at her. "Sit. If I have to bend my neck, it hurts."

She sat in the chair nearest her, one that formed a half circle with another chair and the sofa in front of the fireplace. She perched on the edge of the cushion. "Do you want me to start a fire?"

He started to shake his head, but stopped with a grimace. "Just call and get them to do it."

"Build a fire?"

"Yeah, and while you're at it, ask them for that coffee." He motioned to a phone on a table by her chair. "They'll have it here in ten minutes."

She reached for the phone, but couldn't find a list of numbers to call. "How do you get the front desk?"

"You call the concierge, Alfred. Just push double nine."

She did, and after one ring, a man answered, "Good evening. This is Alfred. How may I serve you?"

"Uh, Mr. Stone would like some coffee," she said.

"The same blend as previously?"

She looked at Cain. "The same blend?"

He said a low, "Yes."

"Yes, that'll be fine."

"Will there be anything else?"

"The fire. Mr. Stone would like a fire lit in the fireplace."

"Cedar or oak?"

She felt foolish but asked Cain, "Cedar or oak?"

He actually smiled. "Let's live dangerously and get both cedar and oak."

She wished her first response wasn't to notice a vague dimple to the right of his mouth, or that her first impulse wasn't to answer the smile. "Both," she said into the receiver.

"Excellent," the man said, as if he was the measure of how everything was done in the world. "Anything else?"

"Anything else?" she asked Cain.

This time there was no smile. "No," he said.

"No, that's it."

She hung up, and clasped her hands in her lap. Cain's eyes were open, but his eyelids were half-lowered, and he was studying her. "You can leave if you want to. I can keep myself awake."

"I'll stay," she said.

"What about your…Sierra?"

"Annie came by at the crack of dawn to take Sierra tree hunting for the perfect Christmas tree."

"I thought Annie was sick."

"She apparently felt fantastic this morning. That was her word. Fantastic. I didn't argue."

"Fantastic is…fantastic," he said with the trace of that smile again.

She looked away, over to the windows and the view outside. The snow was starting up again, and the sun was hidden completely. "Are you sick to your stomach?" she asked, staring at the land outside.

"Nope."

"A headache?"

"Nope."

"Dizzy?"

"Not now."

"Good," she said, and forced herself to look away from the view and back at the man.

"This is kind of nice," he murmured.

"What's nice?"

"Having someone give a damn if you're dizzy or sick or got a headache."

She could give more than a damn about him if she let herself. "I'm just doing what the doctor said."

"Sure you are."

"It's the teacher in me." She made herself sit back and gain more space between the two of them.

"Sure it is," he said softly.

Thankfully, there was a knock on the door, and she scrambled to her feet to answer it. A young man was there with a thermal bag in his hands. "Good evening, ma'am," he said, and when she stood back, he came inside and walked past her, over to a bar. Silently, he took things out of the bag, and by the time she got to him, he was holding a silver thermos and had two red mugs sitting on a simple tray.

"I'm so glad you're here," she said, and he nodded.

"Yes, ma'am."

"The doctor said Mr. Stone couldn't sleep for two hours, and if he gets dizzy or has a headache or anything out of the ordinary, you're to call him. If he gets nauseated, that's not good. And if he passes out or anything, call 911."

That stopped the young man in the middle of taking some shortbread cookies out of a silver container. "Ma'am, I'm sorry. I don't understand why you're telling me all this."

"You came to stay with Mr. Stone, didn't you?"

"No, ma'am, I'm just bringing coffee and setting a fire."

"Oh," she said. "I'm sorry." She'd assumed they'd send the things with whoever would be sitting with Cain. This guy wasn't her salvation; he was just a coffee server.

He picked up the tray and crossed to put it on the coffee table. She went over there, too, but around behind the couch and back to her chair. She sank onto the leather as the man spoke, "Mr. Alfred told me you preferred your coffee black."

"He knows everything," Cain said, and leaned forward to take one of the red mugs the man offered him. Then he eased back in the cushions and rested the mug on his thigh.

The man picked up the other mug and crossed to offer it to Holly. As she took it, he said politely, "Ma'am, if you'd like cream or sugar or anything else for your coffee, I can bring it back."

"Nothing, thanks," she said, wrapping her hands around the warm ceramic.

"Is there anything else, sir?" he asked Cain.

"The fire?"

"Oh—yes, sir," he said, and hurried outside, to reappear in a moment with logs in his arms. While he laid the fire and got it started, Holly felt Cain looking at her. As soon as the door closed behind the man, Holly looked back at Cain. He was still watching her, and she asked something she hadn't intended to. "Don't you have any family at all?"

"Not that I know of."

"Did you…did you ever try to find your parents?"

His expression tightened when he spoke; his tone didn't betray any self-pity. "Why would I? They left me at the orphanage without hesitation. The record said that I was found in the car of one of the caretakers. Someone phoned and told the head of the place to look in the car." He took a sip of coffee, then stared into the mug. "He did and there I was." He chuckled, but it wasn't a humorous sound. "I didn't think that I'd like what I'd uncover if I searched for them."

He was probably right. The pain was there, deep enough the way things were. What if he found his mother and father and they didn't want anything to do with him? Holly was shocked that she felt real anger on behalf of the tiny boy who'd been discarded and had never learned to trust or to be part of anything. "And you…you never got married?"

"No." He sipped more coffee, then put the mug on the table and leaned back again with a sigh.

"Not even close?"

"Not even close," he said, and added deliberately, "and I never wanted it to be any different." He stretched his feet out again and folded his arms on his chest as he rested his head on the back of the couch. He stared at the ceiling. "I never wanted anyone to stay. Life's simpler that way."

She felt a soul-deep ache at his words. It was simpler to be alone? And empty? "Things could change."

"I hope not," he said on a sigh.

She knew it was time to leave. No one should make her feel so sad by his words. She put her untouched coffee on the table and reached for the phone. "I'll call to see when they're sending someone over."

Cain watched her dial the main desk, heard her ask about the doctor's orders, then say "Okay" and hang up. When she glanced at him and said, "They're trying to find someone," he knew that he'd lied to her. He didn't want her to leave at all, but he had never begged a woman for anything in his life. Holly Winston wouldn't be the first. "Go ahead and leave," he said.

She shook her head. "No, the doctor said—"

"Gordie's always been overcautious. Go." He saw her nibble on her full bottom lip, and for a startling moment, he could almost remember her taste. A stupid notion, but real enough for his body to start tightening. He sat forward and rested his elbows on his knees. "You told me once you didn't need a babysitter. Well, I don't need one, either."

She hesitated, then came back and stood over him. And for the first time since they'd met, he felt that she towered above him. "Any headache or sickness?"

He looked up at her, then closed his eyes. "Thanks for all your help. You're free to go." When she didn't say anything, he opened his eyes, taken aback to find her in the chair again. She was watching him with narrowed eyes. "Why aren't you leaving?"

"Why are you mad at me?" Color deepened in her face. "If it's because of what happened in the cabin, I don't—"

"I'm not mad," he muttered as he closed his eyes again.

"I never intended…" Her voice trailed off, then he heard her inhale. "I said it was wrong, and I mean it."

"I get the point."

A knock sounded at the door, and by the time Cain opened his eyes, Holly was on her way to answer it. She pulled the door back and he heard her say, "I didn't think you'd be here."

He turned as Jack strode in, taking his jacket off as he crossed to the couch. He tossed the jacket on the chair where Holly had sat and frowned at Cain. "Gordie tracked me down and I got over here as soon as I could. What in the hell happened?"

"Your bedside manner stinks," he muttered.

"According to Gordie, you stink at being a patient," Jack countered.

"Excuse me?" Cain glanced to his right when Holly spoke. She was barely in his line of sight. "I have to leave."

Jack turned to her. "Gordie told me what you did. Thanks."

"Sure," she murmured, then was out of Cain's line of sight completely. He heard the door open, then close, and he knew she was gone. He didn't have to look. He could feel the emptiness she'd left behind.

Jack pushed his jacket to one side and dropped into the chair Holly had occupied earlier. He sat forward, his elbows on his knees and his eyes intent on Cain. "How do you feel?"

He couldn't tell Jack that he felt empty and it was mostly because Holly had left. That made no sense. "I hurt all over, and my head's no picnic, but I'll survive."

Jack studied him for a long moment, then he asked Cain something that hit him hard. "Would you have made it without Holly?"

He thought he could have made his way back up, or, if he'd had to, eased farther down to where he could get footing. But for a second, he had the strangest question in his mind. *Could he make it without Holly?* And it had no bearing on her saving him earlier. That shook him to the core, and he pushed it away. He could take the risk of wanting her, of maybe not having her. But he couldn't take the risk of needing her. Period. "We'll never know," he said, and sat up to reach for his coffee mug again. The coffee was tepid now, but he sipped some, then put the mug back on the table. "Where were you when Gordie found you?"

"On business," was all Jack said. "So, are you staying here until after the wedding?"

Cain shrugged, and the pain in his shoulder made him grimace. He couldn't drive back to the city now. "Sure. Why not?"

"Joshua and I are getting together tonight. His stepmom is going shopping with his fiancée. I don't have a clue where. So Joshua has some free time. Want to tag along?"

He'd like to see his friend, and right then, it seemed very important to him. "Come on by here and we'll kick back."

"That sounds like a plan," Jack said, then he hesitated. "Can I ask you something?"

"Sure. Go for it."

"What about you and Holly Winston?"

That came out of the blue—at least, it did for Cain. "What about me and her?"

"Malone said you drove her home last night, and then this morning, she's saving your life, and you're here, and not in Las Vegas." Jack shook his head, a slight smile on his lips. "Coincidence? I think not."

Cain sat back. Everything with Holly went fast. From day one. From that moment in the elevator. Time had compressed, but everything seemed bigger than life. Feelings were muddled, and Cain wasn't used to any of it. "She's not one of my fans," he said. "Her husband lost everything they had at the Dream Catcher. She blames me some way, or maybe she just hates anything connected with gambling." He remembered how she'd stopped everything at the cabin. "I can't get it straight."

"What about the land? Did she tell you what she plans to do with it?"

"I told you—it's all she has left of her father. She says she'll never part with it."

"But she's broke."

"I'm sure she's close to it."

Jack considered this for a long moment. "Then she needs money. It's that simple."

Cain didn't argue, but he really felt that there was nothing *simple* about anything Holly did. Jack could think what he wanted to. It wasn't any of his business. "When's Josh coming?"

Jack glanced at the clock. "In an hour or so. Enough time for you to clean up." His gaze flicked over Cain. "Are you sure you're up for this?"

No, he wasn't sure, but he lied. "I'm just fine."

By TEN THAT NIGHT, Jack and Joshua had left after a pleasant evening. They'd ended up sitting around the fireplace in Cain's cabin, talking about the past. Joshua had remembered Old Man Jennings, and they'd laughed at the way he'd run after them when they were on the slope. He'd even remembered Holly. "That little red-haired kid who screeched at us?"

Now Jack and Joshua were gone, and so was the peace Cain had found for a while with his friends. He paced his cabin, confused on so many levels. The last place he wanted to be was Silver Creek, yet he didn't want to leave right now. The last thing he wanted was to be attracted to a woman with a child, a woman who openly disapproved of his life, of what he did. And the very last thing he wanted was to need her.

He wasn't used to being so edgy and confused. He didn't need anything that smacked of commitment or ties. He sure didn't want to be tangled up with kids. And Holly had such a hard time with her ex-husband. Stopping when he and Holly did had been the right thing to do. But it had felt so wrong at the time, and it felt just as wrong now.

Cain stared at the phone for a long moment, then called Jack. "Do you have Holly Winston's phone number?"

There was silence. Jack didn't ask what Cain knew he wanted to. Instead, he gave him the number, said, "Good luck," and hung up.

Cain stood there for several minutes, then lifted the phone again and dialed the number. She answered on the fourth ring, her voice husky with sleep, and every nerve in his body was alive. "Hello?"

"It's me," he said, gripping the phone to his ear. "I just called to thank you for all you did today."

"You…you already thanked me," she said. Just her voice got to him. He closed his eyes. "How are you doing?"

"I'm surviving," he said. "And I owe you."

"No, you don't," she said quickly—too quickly.

He opened his eyes to the empty room around him. He didn't know what else to say, except, "Thanks anyway."

There was silence, then she whispered, "Good night."

"Good night," he echoed, and hung up.

The emptiness around him was oppressive, and he crossed to the bar, poured some brandy, then went to the windows and looked out at the stormy night. Wind drove snow almost parallel to the ground, and the lights from the lifts were barely visible spots of brilliance in the distance.

The mountain was there, but he couldn't see it. The whole

world was there, but he couldn't see it. He took a large drink of the brandy. He felt isolated and singular. He felt alone. For the first time in his life, he hated being alone.

Chapter Ten

Holly stared out her bedroom window at the stormy night. The house was quiet. Sierra was asleep and she was alone. She hugged her arms around herself and imagined it was daylight and she would see the mountain towering over the town. Her mountain—at least, a small part of it. Hers and Sierra's.

No matter how much the wind howled outside, she couldn't get the sound of Cain's voice out of her ears. She closed her eyes and pressed her forehead against the cold glass of the window. Just his voice made her feel more alive, and it made her ache. Stopping what had started on the mountain had been so hard on her, so very hard. Yet it had been the right thing. She knew that logically, but that didn't prevent her from feeling frustrated and uneasy.

"Mommy!"

She turned and hurried to her daughter's bedroom, to find Sierra sitting up in bed, reaching out to her. She caught her in her arms and sat on the bed with her, cuddling her to her, then finally lay down on the bed with her while Sierra fell back to sleep. Thoughts tangled in her mind—the things Cain had told her, the sadness she'd felt at his words. A man alone, a man who seemed to want it that way.

She smoothed her daughter's hair and felt her deep, even breaths. How could a parent give up a child, just drop a child in a truck and walk away? That made her hold more tightly to her daughter, press a kiss to her silky hair. Sierra sighed, deep asleep again, and Holly eased off the bed and went silently to her own room.

She tried to relax, but sleep wasn't there for her. When the phone rang again, she caught it on the first ring. It was almost midnight. "Yes?"

"Hey, baby, it's me." Travis.

She fell back into the pillows. "I hope you're calling to let me know where you sold my locket."

"Can't I just call to talk to you?"

"No," she said flatly, and realized she could hear the familiar sounds of a casino in the background. "Where are you?"

"Having fun."

She sat up, gripping the receiver. Her mother's locket had disappeared just before Holly had left Travis, and until a month ago, he'd sworn he hadn't known anything about it. Then he'd said maybe he could figure out where the locket was if she had some money for him. She'd been broke, and angry, and had hung up on him. "Travis, I—"

"I'm pretty short right now, and I need—"

"Travis," she cut in. "Where is it?"

"Oh, hell," he muttered. "You never give up, do you?"

"Not on this I don't," she said. The last thing she'd given up on was their marriage.

"Okay, okay, it's in a pawnshop."

She'd thought he'd sold it to a friend, or even used it as collateral on a bet. But taking it to a pawnshop seemed even worse for some reason. "How could you?" she demanded.

"Easy," he drawled. "You just go through the door and walk out with money."

"Damn you," she said.

"If you're going to be like that, I—"

"Oh, no, you don't. Where's the ticket for it?"

"Lost it."

"What shop?"

"Don't remember exactly, but it's down on the old Strip. They pay better for some reason."

There were tons of pawnshops in old Las Vegas. And if she had to, she'd go to every one, if they even still had the locket there.

"So, how about it? Can you wire me some money?"

She was proud of herself that she didn't scream into the phone. "I don't have any money," she said simply, and if she did, she'd use it to get the locket back.

"Funny, seems to me that you have one thing."

She closed her eyes tightly. "I need my car, and I need food for Sierra and warm clothes."

"I was talking about your dad's cabin. I heard you got an offer on it, a big offer." She was suddenly cold. He knew about Jack's offer. "Why don't you sell it and we can both live better."

That did it. "I'm tired and I'm trying to sleep. Go back to your fun." She hung up and bit back a scream of frustration.

She finally got up, found the remainder of the bottle of cognac she'd opened when Cain was there and poured some in a glass. She went back to bed, sat up with her back against the cold wood of the headboard and sipped the alcohol. Her locket in a pawnshop. She'd start looking for it tomorrow on the old Strip.

She put the empty glass on the side table and slid down into the bed. She closed her eyes, and thankfully, sleep was there for her. She let go and curled on her side. She was standing somewhere she didn't recognize, her head tilted back, her throat exposed, and someone was slipping the fine chain of her mother's locket around her neck, then fastening it behind her with a brush of warm fingers on her skin. The small heart lay between her breasts, the coolness of the gold welcome on her skin. Then the heat of touch was there again, with aching gentleness. She turned, her lips softly parted with anticipation, and other lips were on hers, tasting her, thrilling her. The locket was caught between her breasts, which were pressed to a muscular chest.

She tasted sleek hot skin, felt a heartbeat under her lips, and she moaned, arching into the embrace. She was dreaming. She knew it. But she went with it. She gave into it, and she lifted her hands, framing a face. Cain's face. She wasn't surprised. It was right. It was what she wanted, his skin against her skin, his body pressed to hers, his hardness an echo of her own desires.

And when he whispered, "Are you sure?" she didn't hesitate.

"I'm sure," she said, and let go of everything.

SHE AWOKE to a cold, harsh morning, with wind whipping around the tiny house and Sierra pulling at her hand. "Mommy, Mommy, hungry," she said, trying to tug her mother out of bed.

Holly blinked at the gray morning light, and although the dream was gone, her body felt as if it had been real. She got out of bed, into the cool air in the house, and her body tightened. "Hungry," Sierra said again.

Holly made herself move and go through the house with her daughter, pushing the dream out of her mind. But it persisted while she made eggs and toast. It was all because of the interlude at the cabin, then Travis's phone call about the locket.

While Sierra ate her eggs and toast, Holly called her sister on the phone in the kitchen. Annie answered on the second ring. "Silver Creek Hotel. Merry Christmas."

"Merry Christmas to you, too, sis. How are you feeling?"

"Tired but okay."

"I was going to ask you if you could watch Sierra while I go back down to the city to pick up a few last things."

"Of course I'll watch her, but I don't think you can get out of town today. The storm's really messed up the roads, lots of ice and that car of yours isn't made for bad weather."

Practical Annie was right, as usual. "Okay," she said. "I'll do it tomorrow, if that's okay."

"Sure. Meanwhile, why don't you both come over? We're going to string popcorn for the Christmas tree."

"Sure, we'll be by in a while."

"Great, see you when you get here," Annie said, and hung up.

By the time Holly walked into the hotel with Sierra, it was ten in the morning, and she still felt off balance. Thoughts of Cain haunted her, but she tried her best to push them away. She stepped into the brass-and-dark-wood lobby, which Annie and Rick had lovingly restored over the years. A wonderful tree already sat by the front windows, and Christmas music filtered in from hidden speakers.

No one was in the lobby. Sierra pulled free and ran toward the desk and around it. "Aunt Annie!" she called, and disappeared in the back. Then Annie was there, smiling at

Holly, Sierra in her arms. Annie looked vaguely pale and tired, but pleased to see Holly. "Hello, there. Come on back. I'm making muffins and getting popcorn popped to put on the tree."

Annie baked the worst muffins, but no one had the heart to tell her that. People dutifully took them, picked at them and got rid of them as soon as they could. Holly didn't have a clue what the guests did with the morning muffins Annie passed out as her guests left to go skiing. Holly followed Annie around the desk and into the living quarters.

The space was warm and comfortable, three rooms—a bedroom, a living room and a large kitchen that used to serve all the guests in the hotel. Now it was divided into halves. One side was still the kitchen, and the other side had been turned into a family dining area. Rick was sitting at the table, a plate of muffins in front of him, and he was cradling a mug of steaming coffee.

"Pour me some of that," Holly said as she sat down opposite her brother-in-law. Annie had made a very good choice in a husband, whereas Holly had made a very bad choice. Rick was terrific and loved Annie dearly. He even ate the muffins. That was real love and devotion.

He pushed a steaming cup of coffee toward Holly, and while Sierra helped Annie pop corn, Holly sipped the coffee and talked with Rick.

"I don't see a barrel of brandy around your neck," he said to her, his mouth twitching with a smile.

"What?"

"I heard you rescued Cain Stone up on the mountain."

She had no idea how he'd heard about that, but she knew that if he knew, everyone else did, too. "He fell and I helped him get back up off a ledge," she said.

"Nice of you to do that," he said. "Given how you feel about the man and all."

He didn't have a clue how she felt about the man, but just talking about Cain brought things to mind that she didn't want there. Annie came to the table with a huge bowl of popcorn and set it down by Holly. "Popcorn-stringing time," she said perkily.

Within moments, the four of them were trying to string popcorn, and Cain Stone was out of Holly's thoughts. Sierra ate as much as she strung, but the laughter around Holly felt wonderful. She hadn't laughed for such a long time. Then all the good feeling ground to a halt when Annie asked, "So, what are you going down the hill for?"

Holly accidentally crushed a puffy piece of popped corn, and dropped the mess on the table in front of her. "Just things," she said.

"I thought you didn't have anything else back there."

Holly glanced at Sierra and Rick, then spoke to Annie. "The locket. Travis finally told me he pawned it. I'm going to track it down and see if I could get it back…or whether I'm too late and they sold it."

Annie was sober now. "That son of a—" She bit off the curse with a quick look at Sierra, then finished with, "How could he have done that?"

"He didn't even think about it," Holly said. "It didn't mean a thing to him but a way to get money for his gambling."

"But it meant so much to you."

Holly shrugged and started stringing the popcorn again. "Well, whatever. I want to find it, then see if I can redeem it. Maybe they'll let me make payments if they still have it. I'll go tomorrow, if that's okay with you."

"Tomorrow's fine," Annie said, but without much conviction.

"If it's not convenient, or if you're feeling sick again...?"

Holly hated to wait any longer, and she couldn't take Sierra with her. When she started to say she'd try to find a sitter, Rick broke in. "I can do the cleaning, and I can take care of the check-in. You go along," he said to Holly, then looked at Annie. "You do too much around here. You're worn-out."

He reached to touch her hand, a simple clasping of fingers, but it made Holly feel incredibly alone. "Thanks," Holly murmured, and knew she needed air. "I have to run over to the school for a few minutes." She glanced at Sierra, giggling at Rick when he put one of the short strings of popcorn around his neck like a necklace. "I can bring her with me."

"Oh, no, she's okay staying here," Annie said quickly.

"Then I'll walk," Holly said, and put her jacket back on. She needed the exertion. She said goodbye to Sierra and left.

Cold air stung her cheeks and forced her to snuggle her chin in her collar. When she got to the parking lot of the school, she saw that the snow was at least two feet deep from the street to the entry of the school.

She trudged toward the front doors, ignoring the snow sneaking into her boots. She almost made it to what she guessed were the front steps, when she heard her name.

"Hey, Holly!"

The sound echoed oddly around her. She turned, and saw a single figure, stark against the whiteness all around, following in her path through the snow. Cain. His head was uncovered, his chin was drawn into the collar of his black leather jacket. His hands were pushed deep in his pockets, and the legs of worn jeans had been tucked into heavy snow boots. She remembered his words about being alone, about wanting it that way, and she watched him, feeling his isolation in the world.

He stopped in front of her, and she saw his wound had been rebandaged with a skin-colored adhesive patch. Smudges of bruising showed at the edges. His eyes narrowed on her. Damn it, she thought. Her heart was beating against her ribs and her hands in her pockets were curled into tight fists.

"I thought it was you," he said.

"Where did you come from?" She couldn't see his car anywhere.

"Gordie insisted on changing my bandage," he said, motioning vaguely with his head back toward the clinic.

"Where's your car?"

"On the other side of the clinic, by Gordie's." He seemed to rock forward slightly. "Did you walk from home?"

"No, I was at the hotel, and…" She bit her lip. "I needed some papers and I needed a walk. Where were you walking to?"

"To you," he said in a low voice, and it startled her.

"What?"

"I saw you out the window of the clinic and walked over."

"Why?"

He shrugged slightly. "Good to see you, too."

She knew she'd blushed at his soft reprimand, but she wasn't up to playing games with him. "What do you want?" she finally made herself say.

He was silent for a moment. "Lunch with you."

She was stunned. "Why?"

"Why not? You saved my life, and you're here and I'm here, and we both eat. I've got a bachelor party tonight for Joshua Pierce, the sheriff's—"

"I know who he is," she said, and remembered the talk around town about his marrying a woman he'd arrested.

"I hate that kind of thing, but Gordie and Jack are set on having one last time together." He looked a bit embarrassed. "I thought we could have lunch."

It unnerved her that having lunch with Cain was tempting. "No."

Now he was the one to ask, "Why not?"

She couldn't say, *Because just being near you makes rational thought impossible and I'm apt to do something stupid.* She remembered too clearly how irrationally she'd acted in the cabin. "I've got a lot to do."

He frowned slightly and spoke a startling truth. "You just don't want to be with me, do you?"

"That's not the question," she said quickly, the color in her face there again.

"I thought we'd gotten past your preconceived notions of me. Besides, all I asked for was a simple lunch. It's not a setup for seduction."

Warning flares shot up each time Cain was near, and as far as seduction went, all he had to do was look at her. No, it wouldn't be a simple lunch. Nothing would be simple with him around. "It's not a good idea. Not after…" She bit her lip. "No, thanks."

He came closer and she felt the snow move around her. "Not after what?" he murmured.

She glanced away, down at the buttons on his leather jacket. "You know," she said, hating the slight breathlessness in her voice.

She was startled when he touched her, his fingers on her chin almost burning her skin. Even though she jerked at the touch, he didn't break it. Instead, he cupped her chin and gently lifted her face so she had to meet his gaze. He had a habit of making sure she was looking at him, and it was just as disturbing now as it had been the other times. "Holly, I stopped everything in the cabin because you wanted me to stop. I have never pushed myself on any woman and I won't. But I find that I would like to get to know you. That's no huge commitment. I'm not into commitments."

He didn't want a commitment. She sure didn't. He wanted to be alone. She had to be alone. She touched her tongue to her lips and closed her eyes. "Just forget it."

The next thing she knew he was kissing her, his lips on hers, his arm around her shoulders, drawing her close to him. The cold and the snow were forgotten, along with why letting him kiss her was so wrong. The contact was fierce and shattering to her. Then abruptly, he broke it, right when she was precariously close to responding despite everything. He let her go, moved back. She opened her eyes to him looking down at her.

Fire was in the depths of his gaze, but he pushed his hands into his pockets. "Forget that, if you can," he said roughly, then he was going, heading back toward the clinic.

She stood there for what seemed forever before she turned to the school and let her hand scrub at her lips. *Forget that, if you can* rang in her mind. *Forget that.* And she admitted with some pain that she probably wouldn't.

She kicked at the snow, found the steps and took them as quickly as the piled snow would let her. She got to the doors, fumbled in her pocket for her keys, then cursed under her breath. She'd left her keys at the hotel with her purse. She turned, and Cain was completely out of sight, but as she went down the steps again, she heard an engine roar to life. A few seconds later, his SUV came into view from around the side of the clinic, smoke curling into the sky from the exhaust.

He got to the street, but before he turned to drive toward the main thoroughfare, he lifted his hand in a half wave. She determinedly kept her hands in her pockets. She waited until he was out of sight before she headed back to the hotel. He'd promised not to seduce her, that they'd just have lunch. That made her laugh, a humorless sound in the cold air around her. Didn't he have a clue how seductive his voice was, how seductive the expression in his eyes, his touch on her skin? "Damn it!" she muttered. Even if he didn't, she did.

When Holly finally got back to the hotel, Sierra and Rick were together in the kitchen, eating gingerbread men. "Mommy! We eated his head," Sierra said with delight as she held up a beheaded gingerbread man.

"I bet that hurt," Holly said with a smile, then looked at Rick. "Where's Annie?"

"She's upstairs with a guest." He eyed her. "You okay?"

"I got all the way to the school and remembered I'd left my keys here."

"Are you going back?"

"No," she said, slipped off her jacket and sat next to her daughter at the table. She picked up a whole gingerbread man and stared at the candies that were supposed to be his eyes. "But I need to check the phone book for some addresses in the city."

"Go on in," he said, motioning to a small office they kept off the kitchen. "Help yourself. Sierra and I will be fine for a while."

She went into the tiny space and got out the Las Vegas

phone book. There were a lot of pawnshops in Vegas, but she chose the older shops Travis had mentioned. They paid best, according to Travis. She found about ten she knew for sure were near the old Strip and began calling. Eight didn't have anything in stock that sounded like her locket. Two had lockets. Both said she'd have to come in to see them. She wrote down the shop addresses, then pushed the paper in her pocket. When she got to the city tomorrow, she'd visit each one. Hopefully, she'd find her locket.

CAIN ACTUALLY ENJOYED the bachelor party. It wasn't like any others. Their closeness was the way it had been with Jack the night before. Old friends sitting around talking, drinking and just being friends. It fit neatly into a place in his life that Cain hadn't known existed until he'd been there with Jack, Joshua, Gordie and Joshua's father. By the time he'd gotten back to his cabin, it was barely ten o'clock and he had the whole night stretching in front of him.

He wished he could have thought back on the past, on the good times with his friends, but the memory that kept coming back was Holly. As much as what had happened at the cabin and later, the kiss in the snow had haunted him. Especially the moment she'd seen him coming toward her in the school parking lot. For a split second he thought he'd seen a smile on her face, a delight at his appearance, then it had gone, to leave him wondering if he'd imagined it all.

But that moment stuck, and he knew it would for a very long time. That second when someone had been happy to see him for no other reason than he was there. Not because he was their boss, or had power or money. Just because he was there. And for a fleeting moment, he'd felt something that he'd never felt before. A feeling of belonging. He'd had it with friends, but it was nothing like this. This was new to him…totally new. Then it had gone. She'd narrowed her eyes on him and refused his lunch suggestion. But he hadn't been able to let it go that easily. He wouldn't let it go.

He reached for the phone, put in the number he knew by heart and listened to the phone ring twice. Then she answered, her voice soft from sleep. He looked at the clock. It was midnight. He hadn't noticed. He started to hang up without saying a thing, but he didn't. "Holly?"

Silence came over the line, drawing out until he said, "Are you there?"

"Yes," came the soft reply. "It's…it's midnight."

"I'm sorry. I hadn't realized how late it was."

"What…what do you need?"

You, he thought immediately, and felt the impact of that admission. But he said, "I just…I was thinking that there's a wedding tomorrow." Words were there of their own volition. "It's at four, at the Inn. Joshua and Riley—they're getting married. I wondered if you'd like to go with me." He was asking for a date—to a wedding, no less—and he couldn't remember the last time he'd actually asked formally for a date.

"I can't," she said quickly, without even taking time to think about it. "I've got things to do. It's so close to Christmas and all. You understand how it is?"

No, he didn't, and he didn't know how it was to get ready for Christmas with a child involved. She obviously paid attention to the holidays, and he hadn't for a very long time. But when he considered it, it was four days to Christmas. No, three days—it was after midnight. "Busy, busy," he murmured, then made himself stop whatever was going on. "Sorry to bother you," he said. "Good night." And he hung up.

He sat in the cabin for a very long time, staring out the windows at the blackness. For a man who knew what he wanted and where he was going, he was sadly lacking in direction. He got up and headed into the bedroom. He'd go to the wedding, he'd wish them well and then he'd figure out what in the hell his future was all about.

If he could.

Chapter Eleven

Cain walked out of the main party room at the Inn at seven that evening. The bride and groom had conveniently disappeared, and the guests were enjoying the champagne and light dinner Jack had arranged to serve after the wedding. He'd had a glass of champagne, talked to a few people, then felt edgy and restless. So he slipped into the main corridor of the lodge, retrieved his leather jacket from an attendant. Then, refusing a cart to take him to his cabin, he trudged through the biting cold, instead.

When he got to the cabin, he changed from his dove-gray suit into jeans and a black turtlenecked pullover. He put on his snow boots and left to get in his car. He drove out the gates of the Inn and headed south toward town. He passed the public lifts and kept going toward the far end of town. He didn't stop until he was pulling up in front of Holly's house. He idled the car at the curb when he realized that all the windows were dark. The house looked and felt empty.

He glanced up and down the street, then drove away. He almost turned right to go down the hill without returning to the Inn, but he hesitated, then swung back to the north. He spotted the hotel, light spilling out the windows and sparkling on the piled snow. He swung into the parking lot at the side of the old building, took a deep breath, almost as if girding himself for war, then got out. He hurried to the side entrance and went into warmth, Christmas music and the fragrance of coffee and cinnamon in the air.

In the lobby, he saw two older people—a couple—sitting near the front windows. Neither of them looked up when he went across the floor toward the desk. Annie walked out of the red curtains at the back, Sierra in her arms. Both she and the little girl smiled when they saw him. He was once again taken aback to realize how much Sierra resembled Holly. The smile. The bright hair. Something in him tightened; then he heard Annie say, "Merry, Merry Christmas, Cain!"

"Maywee Kwismas, Cain," Sierra echoed with a huge grin and a clap of her tiny hands.

"Merry Christmas to both of you," he said as he got to the desk.

"So, how was the wedding?" Annie asked, letting Sierra get down and run around to the front of the desk.

"It's over."

She frowned at that remark. "Well, are we glad it's over?"

"Sorry, I meant that it's…" He shrugged. "It was a perfect wedding."

"Okay, that's better," she said on a laugh.

But before he could ask her about Holly, Annie was peering around him, speaking to the child. "Sierra, no."

He turned to see the little girl trying to take an ornament off the Christmas tree in the lobby.

"They stay on until Santa comes." Cain watched the child hesitate before Annie added, "And if you don't leave the decorations alone, Santa might not want to stop by. Now, that would be just awful, wouldn't it? A Christmas without Santa?"

The child drew back so quickly that Cain almost laughed at her. "That's better," Annie said as Sierra went over to a cupboard near the side entry and opened it to show books and toys, neatly stacked on the bottom shelf. "Just one at a time, Sierra." Then she finally glanced back at Cain. "I'm sure you didn't come to watch Sierra disassemble the decorations?"

"Is Holly here?"

"Sorry, no, she's not here."

"Oh," he said.

"I'm taking care of Sierra for her while she finishes up a few last-minute details." She leaned closer and spelled out *Santa presents,* then said, "And she had a few personal things to attend to."

Annie didn't offer any details, such as where Holly was doing her shopping and taking care of things, so he let it go. "She's staying in Las Vegas?"

"Until tomorrow." Annie frowned again. "Do you know that old area on the original Strip?"

"Sure. Why?"

"Those pawnshops—they're legitimate, aren't they?"

He didn't understand why she asked him that. "What's this all about?"

"I thought you'd know, since you live there and all."

"Know what?"

She hesitated. "Okay, just don't tell anyone, especially Holly, that I told you this, but her ex-husband pawned a piece of jewelry of hers, a gold locket, and she went down to try to get it back. He said it was at one of the pawnshops in the old section. She called around and found two shops that said they might have it, so she's off to check. I'm just worried that they might really pump up the price."

Cain felt real anger toward a man he'd never met. The fool. He'd destroyed so much with Holly. "What shops are you talking about?"

"I'm not sure," she said, her frown deepening just before it cleared. "One was Quick Money something or other, and the other one was a man's name, Jimmy's Pawnshop."

Cain didn't recognize either one, but he had a good idea where they were. "I'm sure she'll be okay," he said. "They're pretty well regulated, especially in Las Vegas."

Annie sighed. "I hope so. Holly's gone through enough without that."

He wasn't sure what else to say, so he said, "I'm on my way down the hill. I just wanted to say goodbye and wish you all a Merry Christmas."

"You aren't sticking around for Christmas? It's only a couple of days away."

"Yeah, and it's busy time for me," he said.

Sierra ran up to the desk and around behind it, lifting her arms to Annie. Her aunt picked her up, and Sierra put her arms around her neck and snuggled into her shoulder. She looked flushed. "Tired, honey?" Annie asked. Sierra just snuggled in more, and Annie looked at Cain. "Merry Christmas."

"Thanks," he said, and knew he shouldn't have come by at all.

He left then, took the time to drive back to the Inn to say his goodbyes, before he headed for Las Vegas. Just after midnight, he got to the Dream Catcher and went straight up to his suite. He slept fitfully, and dawn found him sitting on the balcony off the main room, in the cold, looking down at the Strip, up the way, toward the older section. Pawnshops. He muttered an expletive, then went inside, showered and dressed in Levi's, a pullover and boots and took the elevator downstairs.

Time meant nothing in Las Vegas, and the casino was very active. He worked his way through it, stopping here and there to speak to employees, to have patrons wish him a happy holiday. When he finally got to the garage, he knew he just needed fresh air.

He left his car where it was, walked up the exit ramp, hit the code to put up the security gate and stepped out into the morning. Strutting on the Strip was something that always helped him feel grounded, helped him focus on his life and where he was going. But as he went north, past the other casinos, along sidewalks with people everywhere, the noise jangled his nerves. However, he knew where he was going. To the old Strip.

As he left the main Strip behind he started to walk faster. He cut off Las Vegas Boulevard and into the area that used to be Las Vegas in the old days. He noticed things he hadn't before, mainly the plethora of pawnshops. Small, hole-in-the-wall places that accepted prized possessions and handed over money to lose at the tables. He saw the wear on the buildings, the Closed signs that dotted the neighborhood, the air of seediness that had slowly blanketed that part of the city. Some casinos still made the effort to appear glamorous, with bright lights and an overuse of the color gold, but some of the others had given up and made no bones about appealing to a cheaper market.

He crossed the street to avoid cars going in and out of one casino's valet parking areas, and ended up near one of the shops Annie had mentioned, Jimmy's Pawnshop. He ducked inside. A small man came out of the back. Cain didn't ask if he was Jimmy, just inquired about the locket. The man shook his head and said, "Lockets like that are pretty popular today. Wish I had one."

Holly had been there, Cain thought, and left. Farther up the old Strip, he saw two more shops, then a garish sign that flashed on and off. Quick Money Pawnshop. He headed for it, ignoring a car that honked at him when he cut diagonally across the street. He got to the front window of the shop and stopped.

He saw Holly at the counter. She had her back to him, but no other woman was that tiny, with hair that brilliant in color. She was leaning toward a tall, thin man behind a glass display case, and Cain could feel her tension. She said something to the man, and he shook his head. Holly leaned a bit closer, and Cain thought he could almost see her trembling from intensity when she spoke. The man shook his head again and Holly's shoulders sagged as she pressed her hands to the glass in front of her.

The man said something else, shook his head yet again with what might have been regret, then Holly reached for her purse, which had been lying on the cabinet, and put the strap over her shoulder. She turned to leave, but hesitated, looked back at the man, said something, got a nod this time, and then she headed to the door.

Cain retreated, watching her push the door open and step out onto the sidewalk. She stopped for a moment as if to get her breath, and she never glanced up before she almost walked right into him. He caught her by her shoulders, then her eyes lifted, meeting his, and he could see the start of tears in them. Her face was pale and he heard her gasp as she recognized him. "You," she said in low voice.

He could feel her shaking, and all he wanted was to hold her close and tell her everything was okay. He knew it wasn't, but that didn't stop him from wanting desperately to make things right for her. "Yeah, it's me. Are you okay?"

"Yes, I'm—" She took an unsteady breath, then said, "No, I'm not. I've never been in one of those places before today and they're really awful, horrible."

He wasn't sure how they'd qualify for "horrible," but she obviously hadn't found the locket—or at least, she didn't have it. "You were pawning something?" he asked to get her to talk, and felt her pull against his hold.

He drew back, letting her go, and she said, "No, I was trying to find something."

He'd play this out so she wouldn't know Annie had spoken to him. "Something you pawned before?"

"No, Travis."

"What was it?"

"Just a locket I had." She bit her bottom lip. "It's in there." She started to leave, and he fell into step with her.

He asked something that he already knew the answer to: "You got it?"

"No, I didn't," she said, and his heart lurched at the sadness in her voice. He glanced at her, her head down, her shoulders hunched forward as she walked. "It doesn't matter," she whispered.

He knew a lie when he heard it. He'd told enough himself. The locket mattered to her; it mattered a lot. And her low-life husband had pawned it, no doubt to get money to gamble at the Dream Catcher or some other casino. No wonder she'd thought the worst of Cain at first. He would have thought the worst of himself if he'd been in the same position. They reached the intersection, and she pushed the pedestrian button so she could cross going south. "Where's your car?" he asked.

She stepped off the curb when the signal changed. "At the motel," she said, and hurried across the street.

"What motel?"

She uttered a name and he recognized it. A seedy, worn-out place off the Strip. "I'm catching a cab," he said. "How about sharing it with me."

She stopped and faced him, her eyes meeting his. He was thankful they were on a busy street. If they'd been alone, he wasn't quite sure what he would have done right then. "I can walk it, but thanks."

"That's a long way," he said. "It'll take you half an hour, at least."

She glanced at a slim watch on her wrist. "Oh, shoot. Checkout's at eleven and it's a quarter to now. Damn," she muttered, and went off almost at a jog.

"Share my cab and you'll get there in a few minutes."

That stopped her. She turned to him, and he could see her considering his offer determinedly. Finally, she let out a breath with a shudder and said, "Okay, thanks." But he knew it was the last thing she wanted to do.

HOLLY HAD HAD to brace herself to go into the second shop after the first had been such a bust. She'd spent so much time talking to the shop owner. He had the locket, and he'd shown it to her, but that was as close as she'd gotten. The price the shop owner had tagged it with crushed her joy at seeing it lying in the glass case. There was no way she could afford it. Not even if she made payments.

When she'd walked out the door, she'd run into Cain, and at first all she could think was that if he hadn't been holding her, she would have fallen on her face, that he was an anchor, a safe harbor. Cain Stone, an anchor? A safe harbor? Lunacy was obviously taking over, and she'd proved it even more when she'd told him about the locket.

Now he was at the curb, flagging down a cab for them. If she hadn't been in jeopardy of being locked out of her motel room for not checking out on time, she wouldn't have accepted the ride, no matter how tempting it had been. The cab stopped in front of them, and Cain pulled the door open to let her in. The interior was musty and old, with a hard vinyl seat and a radio that squawked statically as the driver asked where to go. Cain gave the man the motel's name, and the cabbie, who had obviously driven more than a few couples there, gave them a "I know what you're up to look" and said, "Sure thing, buddy," then drove off.

Holly could tell how drained she was when she simply sank back on the hard vinyl and didn't do a thing to tell the cabbie they weren't going to the place for the reason most people did. The motel probably rented by the hour most of the time, and they were strict about checkout, because they probably had someone waiting for a room.

Because of heavy traffic, they arrived at the motel at five minutes after the hour. Holly got out quickly, ready to pay Cain for her share of the cab, but he told the driver to wait and came around to her. "What room?" he asked.

She motioned to where her car was parked. "Right there. Number 110." He went with her toward it, and she wished he'd leave. Then she saw that her room door was open. She hurried over to it. When she swung the door back all the way, she saw a maid busy putting her meager things in her overnight case. "Excuse me," Holly said, and the woman looked at her. "Those are mine."

· "You are late," she said in heavily accented English. "Checkout has passed. You pay more or you leave."

Holly crossed and took the overnight bag from her, pulled the zipper up and said, "I'm leaving."

"Good, good," the woman replied, then started stripping the bed without another word.

Holly glanced around quickly, making sure there was nothing of hers the maid had missed, then turned to go and Cain was there in the doorway. "Everything okay?" he asked as he stood back to let her out.

"Sure. They just have strict checkout policies," she said, heading for her car.

"When you rent by the hour, I guess time is of the essence," he said.

She cringed at his appraisal of the motel, even though it was dead-on. She dropped her bag on the hood of her car and got her keys out of her purse, then opened the car door and tossed her bag onto the passenger seat.

She faced Cain. "Thanks for everything," she said, and fumbled in her purse for her wallet. "Will five dollars be okay for my share of the cab?"

"No, it won't be," he said, and her eyes flew up to meet his, her hand still.

"Excuse me?"

"I've been thinking. I owe you for saving my life." Before she could object, he went on. "How about letting me pay for the cab, and buy you lunch or an early dinner to sort of pay you back for what you did."

"No," she said, pulling her last five from her wallet and offering it to him. "I have to get back."

"Did you get your S-A-N-T-A presents?"

She frowned at him. "What?"

"Annie said you'd gone off to get some S-A—"

She cut him off in the middle of spelling *Santa.* "You talked to Annie?" Annie said far too much to far too many people.

"I went by last night to see if you were there."

"Why?"

"Honestly, I wanted to see you. I feel as if we always get offtrack, and I thought we could have some coffee, talk and figure some things out."

She pushed the five dollars toward him. She didn't want to talk or figure out anything. She had a sneaking suspicion that if she figured things out, it would only make everything worse for her. "I have to get going."

He ignored the bill. "Are you sure?"

Hell, no, she wasn't sure. Not any more than she understood why this man could make her consider things that were off-limits for her. "I have to go," she repeated.

The sun made gold highlights in his hair. "Then I guess that's that," he murmured.

Still ignoring the money, he came closer. "Take care, Holly Winston," he said softly, his gaze dropping to her lips, and for an instant she was certain he was going to kiss her. But he didn't. He simply walked toward the cab.

She went after him, grabbed at his leather jacket sleeve. He stopped and turned to her. She touched his hand, feeling a jolt from the heat there, then quickly pushed the money into his palm. "For the ride," she said, then she hurried back to her car.

She got in behind her wheel, put the keys in the ignition and started the motor. The motor sputtered to a stop. She tried to start it again, felt it crank, kick, then stop again. She sat back, hit the steering wheel with her hand and fought tears of frustration. She didn't need car trouble. Not here. Not now.

A knocking on her window startled her. Cain hadn't left in the cab. He was there, and crouched as she rolled down the window. "Trouble?" he asked.

She covered her eyes with her hands. "No, everything's just wonderful," she muttered through clenched teeth.

She was taken by surprise when the door opened, and Cain's hand caught her by the arm. "Come on," he said. "You're exhausted, and the car isn't about to work. I've got the cab right there."

She held her ground. "I can't just leave my car here," she said. "They'll have it towed or something."

"Get your bag and get in the cab. I'll be right back." After issuing his orders, he strode over to the motel office. When he went inside, she got her things but didn't go to the cab. She headed for the office, too. Before she neared the office door, Cain was coming out. When he saw her, he gently touched her arm to steer her back toward the cab. "It's taken care of," was all he said as he pulled open the back door.

She dug in, stopping them both. "What does that mean?"

"It means that a tow truck will be here soon to tow your car to a garage so they can figure out what's wrong with it."

"Oh, no, I can't—"

"You don't have a choice," he said. "It's not running, and I've never been one of those guys who can look under the hood of a car and figure out what's wrong with it. But I happen to know a man who can, and he agreed to check it for you."

She felt her heart sink. Whatever it cost, she couldn't afford it. But she couldn't afford to be without a car, either. She felt beaten. He was right. She didn't have a choice. She crossed to the cab, pushed her overnight bag into it, then got in after it. Cain slid in with her, and said to the driver, "The Dream Catcher, the side lot, all the way to the back."

Holly stared out the window as they drove, too tired even to think about what she'd have to do. She simply took in the passing view of a city so many called magic, a city that wasn't magic for her. It never had been. Not even at night when the Strip glowed with enough lights to be seen from high in the sky. Day or night, all she saw were the garish golds and reds, the flamboyant buildings that mimicked everything from buildings in New York City and Paris to the pyramids of Egypt and weren't even close to the originals. She'd seen this city over and over again, and the magic had fled almost as quickly as it had come to her when she'd first moved here with Travis. For people like Cain, the city was probably still magical.

The cab slowed, and she saw the Dream Catcher, one of the more subdued structures that crowded the Strip at this end. Three gold-and-glass towers, arranged in a triangle, soared twenty stories into the clear day sky. They glittered like fine jewels, but the fact was they housed a hotel and a casino, just like the others. The cab pulled around into a side lot, past the valet parking, and Cain directed the cabbie to a ramp that slid out of sight behind a heavy security gate.

Cain put in numbers on his cell phone, and the gate went up, allowing access to the underground garage. By elevator doors where Cain's car was parked, Cain paid the driver, then got out. Holly grabbed her bag and followed. He went to the elevator and hit a code panel to one side. As the door slid open, she stopped.

"I can wait in the casino or something."

He glanced at her, his eyes hooded. "No, you can't," was all he said as he reached to keep the door from closing on them.

She ducked past him, into the car, and they rode up in silence, her staring at the door, holding her purse and bag tightly to her middle, Cain beside her. When the car stopped and the door slid open, she was faced with the world of Cain Stone.

His apartment appeared to occupy most of the top floor. There was white marble underfoot, flowing into thick white carpet in a massive living area. A huge expanse of windows showed the Strip snaking off to the north. She hesitated, and Cain touched her arm.

"Welcome," he said, and took her bag from her, then dropped it on a black bench that looked vaguely Oriental. "You're exhausted. Just sit down and rest for a bit. The mechanic will call here when he knows about the car. Meanwhile, how about me ordering up something to eat?"

She quickly stepped out of her shoes, then pushed them under the bench by her bag, removed her jacket and put it on the bench, before lying her purse on top of it. She followed Cain into the living area, her feet sinking into the plush white carpet. Despite the severely tailored appearance of the huge, wraparound white leather sofa that faced the windows, when she sat down into one corner, it felt wonderful.

Black onyx tables framed it on either end, and a huge, free-form coffee table in the same material filled in the U that the sofa's shape formed. Cain came around to sit by her. He leaned forward, resting his elbows on his knees. "What do you want to eat?"

"Whatever there is."

"That's the point. There's anything you want." He studied her. "How about something simple. A ham sandwich and coffee?" When she hesitated, he said, "Hey, you looked after me when I took that fall." He touched the bandage on his fore-head. "Let me look after you for a few minutes."

She wasn't going to argue. She had no strength left to argue. So she nodded, and he got up and went back toward the door. She heard him ordering the food, and she curled up, tucking her legs under her and letting her head rest against the back cushions.

Cain was there again, near her, but that didn't stop her eyes from closing. She'd just relax for a few minutes, she thought, and let go trying to figure out what was happening. Or why she felt so safe and relaxed in this foreign place. She just let go, and slipped into sleep.

Chapter Twelve

Cain sat for a very long time, watching Holly sleep. She'd snuggled into the corner of the couch, her hair brilliant against the white leather. Then she shifted with a sigh, curling to one side, a hand under her cheek, the other lying open on her thigh. He'd never watched anyone sleep. He'd never even thought about watching someone sleep. And the only reason he moved away was there was a soft sound when the elevator door opened.

The waiter pushed the food tray into the suite. With a nod, the man left, and Cain set the cart to one side of the couch. He glanced down at Holly, resisting the temptation to sit with her longer. Instead, he reached for a white-and-black throw that he'd never used and laid it over her. He allowed himself to brush her cheek with his fingers, to feel the silky heat of her skin against his skin, then he drew back. He headed for the office he kept next to the living room.

He worked until the sun was setting and night started to fall on the Strip. Mike the mechanic had called, said the problem was a fuel filter, nothing more serious, and he'd been able to find one, which was now on its way to his garage. He'd have it installed by nine when he closed. Cain had barely put the phone back in its cradle when it rang again.

He answered simply, "Stone."

"Well, Stone," said the voice on the other end.

"Hey, Jack."

"You could have told me goodbye before you made a break from the reception."

"I told Josh and Riley."

"Sure," Jack said, then asked, "Are you coming for New Year's or not?"

"Not."

"I don't suppose you'll cut the cards again."

"No," Cain said, pushing back from his glass-topped desk to face the Strip, which was coming to life. "New Year's is the big one here."

"Yeah, it's the big one here, too," Jack said, and Cain thought he heard something strange in Jack's voice.

"Anything going on you want to talk about?"

"No, just business," he said on a sigh. "Making decisions. You know how that goes."

He did. "Sure."

"I was wondering if you ever heard anything else from Holly Winston."

Cain stared out at the tower—a huge ball lighting up in the night—on the north end of the Strip. "Actually, she's here in Las Vegas."

"What?"

"She's here with me. I'm helping her out."

Jack laughed suddenly. "Well, I've got to hand it to you. Have you worked in a good word that will convince her to sell her land?"

Land? He hadn't even thought about the land. "No, I sure haven't."

"Okay, well, I'm not going to ask how you got her there or what you're doing, but it's appreciated."

"Jack, I'm not—"

"Hell, I have to go. Emergency in the kitchens. Be careful," he said, then hung up.

That was when Cain sensed movement and looked up to see Holly in the doorway to the office.

"I'm sorry. I fell asleep," she said, barely covering a yawn with one hand. Her face was sleep softened, and incredibly attractive right then. She was without guile. No fancy clothes, no perfect makeup, her hair mussed, loosened from her ponytail. Nothing that he was used to at all. Yet Holly Winston took his breath away, even when she yawned again, then shook her head. "Sorry."

He stood and crossed to her, struck by how vulnerable she appeared at that moment. "You really needed it," he said.

She brushed at her hair. "I guess I did."

"Well," he said, fighting the urge to do more than look at her slightly parted lips. "The food's here."

She didn't move. "What about the car?"

"A blocked fuel filter. Mike said he'd have it installed soon." He glanced at the clock. "Another hour or so, and it should be done."

She frowned. "How much is it going to cost?"

"He didn't say, but it won't be too much." Cain would make sure it wasn't. "Right now, I'm guessing that you're hungry, and as I said, the food's here."

She hesitated, then turned and padded back to the couch. She sank down in the corner she'd slept in, tucking her legs under, and looked up at him as he passed by her to get the cart. She'd placed the throw over the back of the couch and rested her hand on it, her fingers playing with it as she watched him.

Meeting her gaze, he knew that doing something mundane at that moment would be good, very good. Anything to distract him from the thoughts that her closeness brought to his mind. He filled two plates with sandwiches and put the plates on the coffee table. "Nothing fancy, but the food's usually very good," he said.

She leaned forward, a wisp of hair falling on her temple, and picked up half her sandwich. Settling back into the cushions, she turned toward the windows and absentmindedly nibbled on the sandwich.

He thought of another mundane thing to do right then. "Drinks," he said, and moved to the bar, where he got out a bottle of red wine, two goblets and a corkscrew. He quickly opened the wine, then carried the glasses and bottle to the table. "It's seven. Time for some wine. Red to go with the ham," he said, pouring them each a glass.

He picked both glasses up and handed one to Holly. She took it from him, her fingers brushing his fleetingly. Yet the contact shot through him with the strength of an electric shock. He sat back, giving himself a bit of distance from her, and cradled the goblet in his hand as he looked to the view.

The Strip was in its full glory now, a sight that never ceased to amaze him. But for the first time since he could remember, something amazed him even more. Holly. She was intoxicating.

"I'll be getting back so late I really need to call Annie and let her know what's going on," she said, and he felt her shift on the couch.

When he looked at her, she was putting her partially eaten sandwich on the plate. He reached for the cordless phone that rested on the sofa table behind the couch and handed it to her. "Help yourself."

While she made the call, he sat back again and watched Las Vegas, while he listened to her talk.

"Is Annie there? It's Holly."

Pause.

"Well, give her the message that I'll be late getting in, but I will be back tonight. I'll call her when I know exactly when."

Pause.

"Thanks. Okay," she said, and he saw her hit the end button and frown.

"Anything wrong?"

She handed him the phone, and as his hand closed on it, he felt her body heat caught in the plastic. "Annie's not there. Probably out doing Christmas shopping or going to that torch show."

He remembered the torch show, some guy dressing up like Santa, and several more guys like elves, holding torches in the night as they skied down the low ridge and right onto the main street, where the Christmas tree was being lit. He'd always known that Charlie's dad was Santa and a pretty good skier. Charlie probably did it now. "Silver Creek does have its traditions," he murmured, then sipped some wine.

"Traditions are good," she said.

He didn't have any, except his fights with Jack over where he, Cain, would spend the holidays. He doubted that would qualify as a tradition in Holly's book. He reached for his sandwich and sat back.

They ate in silence for a while, but it wasn't uncomfortable. It felt good just to be there with her, the Strip spread out below them. Somehow, something in him eased. He had no idea what it was or why he felt it so acutely. "The locket," he said. "Is getting it back in the same category as keeping the land?"

"It was my mother's," Holly said, then finished the last of her wine. "It's what I have left of her, and what I have to give to Sierra from her."

"Does having either thing—the land or the locket—change your memories?" he asked.

He didn't look at her. "No, not really, but it's that connection."

He never looked away from the night. "With the past? With your parents? You're keeping that alive?" He really wanted to know.

"It's part of who I am, what I was."

"If you didn't have either thing, wouldn't you still be Holly?" He sure didn't have anything, but he was still Cain.

He heard her sigh. "You're a philosopher?"

He chuckled roughly. "Not even close," he murmured. Then took a breath. "So, how much do they want for the locket?"

Out of the corner of his eye, he saw her put her glass on the table, then she was out of his sight again. "More than I thought it was worth," she said on another sigh.

"You're going to buy it back?"

"I don't have a choice."

She sounded worn-out with life, and he hated the man who had made her like this. He closed his eyes, but that didn't stop the truth from hitting him right in the middle of his being. Damn it, he *did* care. He really cared. He got up to get more wine.

When he came back to the couch with the opened bottle, she was watching him. The conversation veered off in a new direction, and he was relieved. This topic he could deal with more easily. "Did you decorate this place?" she asked with a sweep of her hand.

He poured more wine into their glasses and said, "Me? No. I paid for this. Where in the hell it all came from I'll never know, but one day it was all here."

"But you paid for it."

"Yes, and they told me white-and-black's the style with punch. It makes the room pop. I don't have a clue what pops or doesn't pop."

She laughed softly, a gentle sound that ran riot over his nerves. "You don't like your own home?"

He glanced around and felt the coldness in what he called home. No, it wasn't a home. It was a place to sleep and work and exist. "I never thought about it before."

"It doesn't look like you," she said.

"Oh?" he said, and glanced at her, his wineglass halfway to his mouth. She'd turned to face him more squarely, her back against the curve of the couch, resting her wineglass on her thigh. "What would look like me?"

She took a sip of wine, then eyed him over the glass. "Maybe something more earth tones, something rich and mellow and casual."

He lifted an eyebrow at her, then took a drink of his wine before he said, "Really?"

"People think you're… No," she said. "I thought you were cold and greedy and evil, I guess." She giggled at that. "Evil. Good grief. Now, that's dramatic, isn't it?"

He found himself asking another question of her, one that seemed immensely important to him. At least, her answer would be important. "What do you think now?"

She leaned forward and put her glass down on the table, and didn't say a thing until she sat back against the cushions. "Now? I don't know. You're human. You're alone. You don't feel connected anywhere. And you have this place, but you never even see it, not really."

Bingo. Her evaluation was spot-on. But she certainly didn't know enough to add that he found her so endearing and so tempting that if he was closer, he'd make a connection with her, and wouldn't stop making it. "I am human," he conceded with naked truth.

She was staring at him and her considering gaze went on for a long nerve-racking moment. In fact, it went on so long that he felt uncomfortable. "What are you thinking?" he finally asked.

She shook her head slightly as if to clear her thoughts, then shrugged before she clasped her hands in her lap. She didn't speak.

"Well?" he asked. "What were you thinking?"

She shrugged again and looked embarrassed. "I was just thinking that you…after all that happened with you, you really did well for yourself. Everyone knows Cain Stone."

That wasn't what he wanted to hear, not from her. "Cain Stone doesn't exist. It's just a name they gave me." He shocked himself by saying those words, and he was just as shocked by the tinge of bitterness in them.

When she rested her hand on his arm, he was startled, and his whole body tensed at the contact. God, he didn't want sympathy from her. Not from her. "You're who you are, not what you're called," she said softly.

Who was he? What was he? He glanced down at her hand on his forearm, and her slender fingers felt warm. Right then, all the physical desire he experienced for Holly was overshadowed by something else. For the first time ever, he sensed a solid connection, one he didn't even have a name for.

HOLLY WAS STUNNED that she could feel a pain in Cain, a pain that seared through her, leaving a need to blunt it. She leaned toward him, someway trying to ease that pain in him. All she wanted to do was to make his pain go away, but there were no words she could offer, so she simply held on to him.

Then he lifted his hand and touched her cheek, and she was drawn closer. She pressed her hand to his heart. It thudded against her palm, beating strongly, "I'm sorry," she whispered, not at all sure what she was sorry for.

He grimaced, then groaned "Oh, God" and reached for her, gathering her into his chest.

They sat together for what seemed an eternity, her hand pinned between them. He held to her and she held to him, and she wasn't at all sure why she couldn't let go. She didn't want to let go. Finally, he eased her back, looked down into her face with shadowed eyes, and she was very sure in that moment why she wasn't pushing back, why she wasn't freeing herself from his hold. She wanted this man. Wanted to be with him, to touch him and have him touch her. There was no logic in it, just pure need, and when his lips lowered to hers, that need exploded in her. A hunger sprang to life. Any thoughts of why she shouldn't be going to this man fled. She tasted him, felt him. His hands were on her, and she felt skin against skin, his caress, his touch, like fire on her skin. She arched toward the contact, moaning softly, and his lips found her nipple. She had no memory of her top being undone or her bra being pushed aside. All she knew was the pleasure licking through her, the desire flooding her, and Cain everywhere.

He was by her, then over her, his lips trailing along her skin, replacing his hand on her breast, tugging at her nipple, drawing ecstasy through her. The closeness was like it had been at the cabin, suddenly there, suddenly right, and when he whispered her name, she kissed him. He moved on her, and she felt his hardness. She fumbled with his belt and the button on his jeans.

The zipper was down, and he pushed with one hand, holding himself to one side and while he lowered his jeans, set himself free. She felt him through the white cotton of his briefs, and she heard him groan at her touch. He arched back, then moved closer, his lips on her throat. Then his hand was at her waist, at the fastener for her jeans. The snap undid quickly, and he pushed the jeans down, splaying his hand on her abdomen, going lower. The only important thing was that next instant, that next touch, that sense of pleasure and joy.

Then suddenly the phone rang, a strange double ring that stilled Cain's hand on her and broke the moment. He eased right, then whispered, "Let me get it and get rid of them."

She shifted toward the back of the couch, letting their legs untangle, then he was sitting by her, his hair mussed, his eyes smoldering on her as he reached for the cordless phone. He flipped it open and said, "What?" abruptly.

He listened, then said, "Of course," and turned to her, holding out the phone. "It's for you. Annie."

"Me?" She scrambled up, suddenly needing to be covered, but not taking the time to get her clothes back in a semblance of order when she saw his dark, concerned frown.

"When you called your sister, my number came up on the caller ID, and you weren't answering your cell phone so Annie phoned here."

She took the phone from him and pressed it to her ear. "Hello?"

Annie spoke, but it was an entirely different Annie from

the one Holly had left Sierra with yesterday. This Annie sounded upset. "Holly, it's Sierra. She's sick, really sick. We're at the clinic with Gordie. She had some sort of seizure."

Holly felt the bottom drop out of her world, and for one second, she thought she'd faint. Then the world screeched to a horrible stop. "What is it? What's wrong with her?"

"Gordie isn't sure. He's doing a blood panel and whatever else he can do here. She's got a high fever, and she's…" Holly felt terrified when she heard her sister sob softly before managing to say, "I don't know what happened. She was fine one minute, then she was burning up and—"

"I'll be there as soon as I can."

Holly stood, placed Cain's phone on the table and reached blindly for her clothes. With awkward motions she put them on, choked by panic but trying to keep control. "What is it?" Cain asked. "What wrong?"

She told him as she dressed, then crossed to get her boots and jacket on. "I have to get back."

He was behind her, talking, and she realized he was speaking on the phone. She turned to see him frowning as he asked, "Is it doable?" He nodded. "Good. Stand by and we'll be there in—" he glanced at the wall clock "—give me ten minutes and be ready to go the instant we arrive."

He hit the end button, dropped the phone on the couch and came over to her. He grabbed his leather jacket and shrugged into it while she grabbed her purse and her overnight case off the floor. Then he looked down at her. "Let's go."

As much as she desperately wanted to hold on to someone or to have someone hold her up, she couldn't ask Cain to make that trip. "No, I need to drive back there now."

"You can't. Your car's not ready, as far as we know."

God, she hadn't remembered her car until he'd spoken. "Oh, no," she breathed. "Then I'll…I'll rent one."

"No, you won't. I'll get you there as fast as possible." He took her arm without saying anything more, grabbed her bag out of her hand and led the way to the elevator. In moments they were in the parking garage, climbing into his car. He drove up the ramp, out into the parking lot, then out onto the Strip. But he headed south, the opposite direction from home.

"We're going the wrong way," Holly said, clutching her purse so tightly in her lap that her fingers were almost numb.

"We're going to McCarron." The airport served all of Las Vegas and the surrounding areas. "My helicopter is waiting to take us back to Silver Creek."

Given her anxiety, all she could do was go along with him. Then he touched her hand, warmth in that touch, and he said softly, "Trust me. I'll get you there."

And he did.

He sat by her in the helicopter, holding her when she started to shake and telling her that they'd be there soon. Within an hour they were driving out of the Inn in a car Jack had had waiting for them at the helicopter pad, which had been totally cleared of snow. Cain drove into town as quickly as he could, pressing the horn more than once to get people to move out of the way. When he reached the clinic, Holly was out of the car before it even stopped and was running for the door.

She raced into the main waiting room, white and sterile looking. Annie was there, coming toward Holly, her arms out. Annie held on to Holly for a moment, then whispered, "It's going to be okay. It's going to be okay."

But when Holly drew back, she could see the paleness in her sister, her shaking hands. "Where's Sierra?" she asked.

Annie led the way to the back of the clinic, to a four-bed patient room. Only one bed was occupied. Holly ran over to it, and her heart wrenched at the sight of her daughter, so tiny, so still under white cotton sheets. One tiny hand lay on the top of the sheets and a tube from an IV drip was attached to it. "Oh, my God, please," she breathed, the prayer she'd been saying since receiving the phone call.

She sat on the bed and touched Sierra's face. The little girl didn't respond. Her eyes were closed, her auburn lashes stark against her pallid skin. Holly stared at her chest raising and lowering, watching each breath her daughter took. Then Sierra shifted, making a small, crying sound. Holly got onto the bed with her and carefully gathered her daughter into her arms. She lay with her, speaking softly to the child, trying to ignore the unnatural heat of her skin. "It's okay. Mommy's here, sweetheart," she murmured, and when the tears came, she didn't bother to wipe them away. "I'm here. I'm here."

At first Holly didn't realize anyone else was there, then she saw Gordie go to the other side of the bed, check something by the IV. He spoke in a low voice. "Her temperature is still high, but it's easing some. And there haven't been any more convulsions."

"What is it?" she asked, then realized Cain stood off to Gordie's left. She met his gaze, and in that moment, she felt a sense of comfort. It had come out of nowhere, and grew stronger when he spoke to Gordie.

"Does she need to get to a hospital?" he asked the doctor.

"If we can't break her fever soon, she should be transported to a place that's better equipped for pediatric emergencies."

"My helicopter's at the Inn. Just let me know if you need it for her. Or to fly in a specialist."

Gordie considered what Cain had said, then shook his head, "If the fever goes up again, we'll do what we have to do. I think we have to give her a bit of time. It would be pretty hard on her to make a move right now."

Cain met his gaze directly and asked what Holly had been thinking. "Are you positive?"

Gordie nodded. "For now." He looked down at Holly. "We'll give her two hours. If there's no change or if things…" He hesitated. "In two hours, we'll make a decision."

Holly closed her eyes and clung to her daughter. Then someone touched her cheek, and she looked up to find Cain bending over her. "I'll be here," was all he said, then he left with Gordie.

"I'll be here." His words sank into her being and she held on to them as tightly as she held on to her daughter. He'd be here. He'd be here.

Chapter Thirteen

Cain paced in the hallway outside Sierra's room, fighting the urge to look in every couple of minutes. When he did, it killed him that there was nothing he could do to make it better. He could almost feel Holly's pain as she cradled her daughter. He finally went to speak to Gordie about this, but Gordie was nowhere to be found.

Cain went into the rear of the clinic, and saw Gordie coming in from the rear door, his jacket pulled around him. "Where were you?" Cain demanded, and Gordie stopped in his tracks.

"Getting a book out of my car," he said. Cain saw a thick book he held in one hand. "Is something wrong?"

Everything, Cain thought. "I just wanted to know if there wasn't something else that could be done for Sierra."

"We're waiting," Gordie said evenly. "I've done all I can do right now. When the blood tests get back, maybe we'll have more to work with, or maybe we'll have to get her out of here." He frowned, and Cain realized this was hard on the man, too. "Give me a broken leg on a stupid skier any old day," he said as he handed the book to Cain to hold while he got out of his jacket. He dropped it on a desk in the hall, then took the book back. "It's harder with kids."

"How much longer do we wait?" Cain asked.

Gordie checked the wall clock. "Half an hour. Tops." He studied Cain. "You're pretty attached to the child, aren't you?"

The question stunned him, and all he could do was nod. He hadn't realized that because Sierra was Holly's daughter, she was included in his feelings. Whatever they were, the little girl was in the mix, and that rocked him. He'd never cared about a child in his life. But now… "I'm worried about Holly."

"Yeah," Gordie said, glancing past him at the door to the room. "Me, too."

A nurse called to Gordie, "Doctor? It's Ellen Raines on the phone. It's about Dougie."

"Broken collarbone from snowboarding," Gordie said, then clapped Cain on the shoulder. "Be right back."

Cain watched him go into the waiting room, then crossed to the door. He eased it open and saw Holly still on the bed with Sierra. Neither was moving, and he waited to see each of them take a breath. He felt like an intruder in their lives, but he couldn't just leave. Gordie was correct. He was getting attached, and he wasn't sure where that was leading. For now, all he wanted was to see Holly smile again—that meant Sierra would get better. He wanted it a lot, no matter what it cost him.

He backed out and heard voices in the waiting room. He went in the opposite direction from them, into a hallway, to stairs that he remembered so very well from his childhood. He went up them slowly, and at the top reached instinctively for a light switch, which was still in the same place it had been over twenty years ago. The dull overhead light illuminated a dingy hallway lined with boxes of medical supplies and unused equipment.

He walked down the hallway, into his past, to the door of his old room, paused, then pushed it back. The shadows were touched by a light from the outside, maybe a streetlamp, and the space was empty. No bed against the wall, lined up with two other beds. No dresser where he got one drawer for himself. No green paint on the walls; now they were a dull white. He stared hard at the space, then turned his back on it and went out, closing the door behind him.

The Cain Stone who had left here alone, without any idea where he'd go or what he'd do, was back, no clearer now about his life than he'd been then. He stopped and leaned against the closed door. No, that wasn't true. There was Holly. He shook his head. What about Holly? He cared about her. Damn it, he really cared about her. But did that change what he was and what his life was going to be? What his life could be?

In that moment, a man who had never resorted to prayer prayed it did. He wanted her in his life. He wanted her to make a difference for him. He wanted her. He looked around, at this place where there had been coldness and loneliness. But Holly was with her daughter, and now there was love and caring—the exact opposite of what he'd had here. He stood and slowly went downstairs, to where Holly was with Sierra.

His hand went out to touch the door to Sierra's room, then he drew it back. What he needed and what was reality were two different things. What he wanted and needed wasn't relevant at the moment. It was what the child needed. He knew that what he needed didn't count. Not here, not now. It was what the child needed.

Gordie appeared back in the hallway and held up a hand to him. "I was just going in to check on Sierra." He came closer and motioned to the door. "Let's do it."

Cain hesitated, then pushed back the door. Holly was there, but sitting up, and Sierra was in her lap, her tiny head resting against her mother's chest. Holly looked up as they entered the room. Her face was wet with tears, and he could see she was shaking. His heart plunged. "What—"

Then the most remarkable thing happened. Holly smiled. Really smiled. A smile that lit up her face. And she said in a low, unsteady voice, "Her fever. It's…it's gone. I think it's gone."

Gordie hurried around Cain to the bed and started checking the child, who stared up at him with those huge eyes so like her mother's. Cain stayed back, giving him room, watching him and watching Holly. Then Gordie stood straight, pushing his stethoscope into the pocket of his white jacket and clapped his hands. "Her fever broke. It's down to a hundred even." He touched Sierra on her head, her damp hair clinging to her skin. "She's out of the woods."

"Are you sure?" Holly asked softly.

"Absolutely. What she needs now is sleep, and so do you," Gordie said to Holly.

"I'll stay with her," Holly said.

Gordie didn't argue. "Of course. I'll get Clara to bring in some extra blankets." He touched Sierra on the head again. "If she stays like this, you can take her home in the morning. Just in time for Christmas."

"Thank you," Holly said, and Sierra snuggled into her. Then Holly looked past Gordie at Cain. "Thank you."

He nodded and watched Holly scoot back on the bed with Sierra and curl up with her on the pillows. He hesitated, killing an urge to help her with the blankets. Gordie did. Gordie settled the two of them. Then the door opened and Annie and

Rick were back. They moved past Cain as if he didn't exist and went to Holly and Sierra. There were voices of happiness, some more tears, and Cain realized it was time to leave. Sierra and Holly had family. They had support. They had love.

Gordie touched his arm and led the way out of the room. The door closed behind them, and Gordie released a huge sigh. "Boy, am I relieved she's going to be okay. The blood tests didn't show a thing. Nothing."

"Then what happened?"

He shrugged. "As crazy as it sounds, kids her age can get fevers for no apparent reason, and girls, more then boys, tend to get fever convulsions. That's what I think happened. I'm just no pediatrician, and I was winging it a bit."

Cain tried to smile. "And they call medicine a science," he murmured.

"Yeah, they do, don't they. It's that and heck of a lot of guessing and luck," Gordie said, then frowned at Cain. "You look beat. You need some sleep, too."

Cain wasn't sure he could sleep. "Yeah, I guess so."

"Are you sticking around or—"

"You're letting her take Sierra home in the morning?"

"As long as things go well, sure."

"Hey, you two!" Cain turned and Jack came toward them from the front area. "What's happening?"

"Sierra's going to be okay," Gordie said.

Jack appeared harried, his hair mussed, his jacket undone. "Great, great!" He looked at Cain. "How about you? I've never seen you so worried."

Cain shrugged. "I'm fine."

"So, what are you doing?"

Cain shook his head. "I don't know. Holly's staying with

her daughter for the night, and Gordie says he's sending the child home tomorrow."

"Your cabin's waiting for you if you want it."

"I should be heading back."

"If you're thinking of flying, the pilot said he's grounded for now. It's snowing again."

He exhaled. "Okay, I'll take the cabin." He glanced at the door, then at Gordie. "Let me know if things change at all."

"You got it," he said, then went back into the room. When the door opened, Cain heard some laughter and Holly saying, "I can't believe it," then the door shut and he was on the outside.

He left with Jack, went back to the Inn, back to the same cabin and back to doing what he'd done his last couple of nights there. He sat in the darkened living room, nursing a brandy and watching the night. Sleep didn't come easily, and that night, it didn't come at all.

When dawn broke, Cain stood and stretched, went in to take a shower and find some clothes he'd left there. After discarding the bandage and leaving the healing cut uncovered, he was on his way to get his jacket, when the phone rang. It was Gordie, and Cain felt his heart lurch. "What's wrong?"

"Nothing, nothing," Gordie said quickly. "Sierra's fine. But Holly's exhausted and she won't even go home to change. I'm keeping Sierra here until this afternoon, just as a precaution."

"What do you want me to do?"

"You seemed close to Holly last night, and I thought you might be able to talk her into going home, at least changing clothes and getting something to eat."

He didn't hesitate. "Okay, I'll try," he said. "I'll be there in a few minutes."

He hung up, then called Jack and said he'd need the car a bit longer. Jack got the update on Holly and Sierra, then said, "So, you're sticking around?"

"For a few hours. If the snow doesn't stop, I'll drive to the city. If not, I'll fly back."

"Okay," Jack said. "Just keep me up-to-date."

"Talk to you later," he said, and grabbed his jacket to leave.

HOLLY SAT with Sierra while her daughter slept. The little girl was cool now and her breathing was easy. With everything that had gone on since Holly had left Silver Creek a day ago, she felt drained. But thankful. And grateful. She also felt tired. Really tired.

She went to get a drink of water as the door opened. Cain stood in the doorway, weariness at his eyes and mouth, too. The wound on his forehead appeared to be better, though the skin was still bruised. He glanced at Sierra. "She's okay?"

"Yes, yes," she said, and crossed to the tiny bathroom off to one side. She drank some cool water, then went back into the room. Cain was by the bed, staring down at her daughter. She went closer. "She's so tiny," she whispered. "I don't know what I would have done if—" She bit her lip to cut off the words before they could come to life. "She's going to be okay."

Cain turned to her, and inches separated them. He was close enough for her to inhale a fresh soapiness about him, mingled with the leather of his jacket and the scent of the cold and snow outside. She had a flashing memory of being in his arms, of being held and touched, but she quickly suppressed it, and went to sit down in a chair by the bed. She watched Sierra. "She's going to be fine," she said, as much for herself as to tell Cain.

"Gordie says she is," Cain said, then his hand touched her shoulder. "Listen, you're beat. You need to get something to eat, have a shower, change your clothes."

"I can't—"

His hand tightened on her just a bit. "Yes, you can. Annie's on her way and she'll stay with Sierra. You'll just be down the street. You could run here if you had to. But you won't have to."

She couldn't take her eyes off her daughter, or ignore Cain's touch on her shoulder. "What if—?"

"No 'what ifs,'" he said. "Come with me. I'll drive you to your place. You can freshen up, eat and be back in an hour or so."

She almost felt that if she left, things would crash and burn for Sierra. Then she realized it wasn't Sierra she was worried about; it was herself. She didn't know if she could hold herself together if Sierra wasn't there. Then Annie was coming into the room. Annie was hugging her, brushing at Sierra's sweet face, smiling at Cain. "Get her out of here," she said to the man.

"I'm trying," Cain said, his hand lingering on her shoulder.

"Sis," Annie said. "Go. I promise I'll stay right here. And if…and I don't think this will even happen, if something changes, I'll get you right away. You're two minutes away."

Holly hesitated, then made herself let go. She leaned over Sierra, kissed her cheek, then stood and said, "Okay, just for a while."

"You have some food and you'll feel better," Annie said.

Cain was there, and she was grateful that he didn't release her until she reached for her jacket. He had the jacket and was easing it over her shoulders. Then his arm was around those shoulders, and she went with him.

She got into his car parked by the side door, and he drove her just down the street. She knew if she'd had to walk the distance she wouldn't have made it. But when he stopped in front of her house, she couldn't get out. "I can't do this," she said, taking her hand off the door handle. "Just drive me back."

"Why?" he asked, shifting to face her as the car idled.

"What if I'm in the shower and the clinic calls? What if I don't hear the phone ringing?"

"I'll stick around and listen for the phone," he said, and turned off the car.

She didn't realize what he was doing until he was at her door, opening it and reaching in for her. He circled her waist with his hands and lifted her out of the car. She expected to feel her feet plunge into the newly fallen snow, but that didn't happen. He carried her all the way up to the porch, up the stairs and to the door. That was when he put her down. "Get your key," he said, and she fumbled in the purse she'd been gripping and found the key.

He took it from her hand and unlocked the door, then touched her shoulder to urge her inside. He went in with her, into a house that was painfully empty without Sierra. When she turned to thank him, he was closing the door behind her. He'd meant it; he was going to stay and listen for her phone. He studied her for a long moment, then waved a hand. "Go have a hot shower and relax. I'll be right here all the time."

Her "Thank you," was barely audible before she went into her bedroom, closing the door behind her. She eased off her clothes, stripping down on the way to the bathroom, then flipped on the water and stepped under the stream as soon as it heated up. She lifted her face to it and felt everything in her dissolve. Tears came, hard tears, and she let them fall. Sierra was fine. And Cain was right there. Everything was okay.

When she finally stepped out of the shower, she felt drained but in a good way. All the knots and aches in her soul were unwinding, and she could actually breathe again. She towel-dried her hair, then left it loose and curling around her shoulders. She dressed in jeans and a white sweater. When she stepped back out into the living room, Cain was by the front windows, staring out at the street. He must have heard her enter, because he turned to meet her gaze.

"Better?" he asked, not moving.

"Better," she said.

"How about something to eat?"

"I don't know if—"

The phone rang then, cutting off her sentence, and she hurried to pick it up. "Holly?"

It was Annie. "What's happened?" she gasped.

"Someone wants to talk to you." Then Sierra's voice was on the line. "Mommy, I wuv you."

Holly bit her lip hard, and could barely manage to say, "I love you, too, sweetheart."

"Santa's comin'," the little voice said. "He's got a big huge present for me."

Then Annie was back on the line. "She's doing great, honey. Just great. You take your time. Santa, aka Charlie, is coming by the clinic, and Sierra's all excited about it. So am I." Annie laughed softly. "I'll call you later and tell you when you can come and we can take Sierra home."

"Thank you," Holly said, and hung up the phone.

Cain was behind her. She felt him before she heard him. "What is it?" he asked, his voice a rumble at her back.

Holly turned, not aware she was crying at all. "She's fine. She's okay. She's—" He voice broke on a sob, and Cain had her in his arms.

What had felt right in Las Vegas felt perfectly right then. Cain being there. Cain holding her. She tipped her head back, and his hand moved to brush at her wet cheeks. He gazed down at her. "I wish—"

She waited for him to continue. When he didn't she asked, "What do you wish?"

He was still for a long moment, then he lowered his head to hers. "This," he breathed simply, and kissed her.

There was no hesitation in her at that moment. Her mouth opened in invitation, and she was in his arms. She curled into him, her arms around his neck, and she felt him lift her high so her legs could wrap around his waist. There was no stopping this time, no stopping at all. She'd begun it and she'd finish it. She'd have Cain with her, and she'd love him. She loved him. The thought settled in her, and she knew it was a basic truth in her soul. She loved him.

She tasted him, felt his hands circle her, and he was carrying her with him. They were in the darkened bedroom, still steamy from the shower, and he took her to the bed. Together they went down onto the linens, and they didn't let go of each other. Holly couldn't let go. She was almost afraid that if she did, he'd leave. And she desperately didn't want that to happen.

He eased over her, supporting himself on one elbow to look down at her, and she found she could smile up at him. The expression was shaky but real, and she touched his face. She felt the angle of his jaw, then the heat of his lips, and she trembled. How could she love him so completely, so quickly? It stunned her, but it was right, very right.

"If you want to stop," he whispered roughly, "tell me now, because if you don't, I'm not responsible for what I'll do."

She stroked his cheek, then brushed her fingertips to the hollow in his throat. "No, don't stop," she breathed. "Please don't stop."

She had thought their joining would be frantic and needy. She'd felt so tied up with a need for him since the first, but it came slowly and gently. She helped him tug his sweater over his head, then kissed his sleek chest, relishing the guttural sound in his throat when she found his nipple with her tongue. She tasted him, storing away sensations and feelings, and touched his heart. She felt it beating against her palm. She loved the connection, then eased back in the bed as he caught the hem of her sweater and pulled it up.

The soft wool gone, Cain reached for her, easing her to her side so he could undo the snap on her bra. Then the lace was gone, and her breasts swelled at his touch. His lips teased her nipple, and his hand stroked down to her stomach. His fingers tucked under the waistband of her jeans. She moved, pulled the fastener open and lifted her hips when Cain got onto his knees to pull the denim off her, before tossing it on the floor by her sweater.

Then he was over her, looking down at her, and she felt her whole body ready itself for his touch. It came, and his hands stroked her skin, his lips tracing kisses on her. When she lifted her hips to him this time her panties were gone, and she knew that she only wanted skin on skin. She tugged at his pants, then he was gone. He was off the bed, standing in the shadows, removing his pants, and he stood there, his briefs barely containing his hardness.

She reached out to him. He came to her but didn't get on

the bed. He stood near enough for her to take his briefs most of the way down. He finished taking them off himself and she had a glance of him over her before he lay down with her. She realized he had protection in hand. He undid the foil pack, put it on before he rolled toward her on the rumpled linens.

Whatever slow pleasure had been building, it was blasted away in a white-hot flare of passion between them. Close wasn't close enough. Touching wasn't touching enough. Kissing wasn't kissing enough. Then Cain was between her legs, feeling her, testing her, and then he entered her. He settled deeply in her, and the world stood still. Neither of them moved; Holly barely breathed. Then Cain drew back and every nerve in her body was alive.

He thrust into her, and she lifted to him, over and over again, wishing she could melt into him, become a part of him. The sensations grew and grew, and right when she thought she couldn't bear it any longer, she had her wish. She became one with Cain, in every sense of the word, and she was complete. She was in a world that was so perfect, so right. She held to it, not about to let go of it even when he left her and pulled her to his side of the bed. She held on to it and closed her eyes.

CAIN STARED into the shadows, his world changed from what it had been before he'd made love to Holly. Nothing was the same—not him, not what he wanted, not what he needed. The idea that he loved her nudged him, then he gave in to it, and found that he could admit he loved her with an ease that took his breath away. Against all odds, he could love. He did love. He loved her. If she'd been awake, he would have told her over and over again that he loved her. That Cain Stone, the gambler, the man who had never even suspected that love really existed, had found it. What were the odds? he thought. A million to one? Maybe so. And maybe he was the luckiest man in this world.

He felt her snuggle more into him as he held her, and he stroked her arm that lay on his stomach. She shifted again, one leg going over his thigh, lying there heavily, and it felt wonderful. Then he felt her hand move on his stomach and she sighed deeply. She'd been sleeping for at least an hour, but he could tell she was awake. Knowing that, he also knew that his body had started to respond to her touch, to her fingers trailing over his skin, going lower, even though he'd thought he was sated.

He heard a soft chuckle, and he closed his eyes as she circled him. "Awake?" she whispered against his skin.

"Mmm," he managed.

"Good," she answered softly, and shifted away from him.

"Do you have more protection?" He rolled onto his side, found his pants and retrieved the packet. He lay back down and let Holly take care of it for him. Then she was over him, straddling him, and with exquisite slowness, she eased down on him. He filled her, and the explosion of sensations took his breath away. She moved, and they built. His hands circled her waist, lifting her partly, bringing her back to him, and she arched her back, gasping. He captured a breast in one hand and he felt her tighten on him reflexively, and they both gasped at the same time, both climaxed at the same time. Then Cain sensed Holly slowly come closer, to lie on his chest, her hair tickling his skin.

"Oh, goodness," she whispered, and she looked into his eyes. "Oh, my goodness."

"Oh, yes," he said.

She shifted, and he was out of her. She was by his side again, her hand on his heart. "Thank you," she breathed.

He held her tightly against him, kissed her hair, then said, "Holly?"

It was her turn to say "Mmm?"

"I was going to…"

She shifted, settling more against him, and she sighed deeply. He inhaled the scent of her and stroked her arm. Her skin was like silk infused with heat. It was the way her body had felt on his. Heat and silk. He pressed a kiss to her hair again and said, "Holly, I love you."

There was silence, then a soft snoring. She was asleep. There was time enough for them, he thought. Time enough for him to tell her that he loved her and make her believe it. All the time in the world, if she'd have him.

Chapter Fourteen

Holly awoke with a start, alone in the bed. The space beside her was empty. She quickly got up, grabbed at her robe and put it on as she went out into the living room. But Cain wasn't there. That was when she heard a sound in the kitchen and smelled coffee brewing. She went to the swinging door between the rooms, ready to push it back and see him. There was so much to say, so much to find out. Neither one had spoken about love, but she knew she had to. She had to tell him. And whatever happened, happened.

She heard his voice—he was obviously speaking on the phone to someone and his tone stopped her dead. "I told you—I'm with Holly now. I'm going to take her back to the clinic, let her get her little girl, then we'll talk. I can't talk about this now. There's too much going on to think about it. It wouldn't work."

He sounded tight, as if he was stressed, as if the person on the other end was pushing him. She frowned. "I told you—I have to talk to her and get things settled, then I'll know about the land."

He exhaled harshly. "Listen, I said I'd get an answer for you. You'll have the land. Just give me time. I need to go." A pause. "Yes, I realize it's important. It is to me, too." Another pause, then, "Later."

Holly felt her world start to tilt again, but this time it had nothing to do with her child. Cain. He wanted the land for Jack. He'd wanted it all along. All the time. She pressed a hand to her stomach to control the sickness there. All the time.

The door moved and Cain was there, right in front of her. He reached out to her, and she jerked back, unable to bear even him touching her again. She'd made mistakes before, horrible mistakes, but something in her sensed that this mistake with Cain would come close to being lethal. "It was always the land, wasn't it? You and Jack. The builders, the takers."

"What—"

She could feel fire in her cheeks. "I heard you. It was always the land. Always. You and my father and that damn land!" She was screaming now and she didn't care. "I thought you cared about…about Sierra and helping me, and all the time, you were just getting closer and closer so you could spring your trap." She swallowed hard and watched his face tighten until he was almost unrecognizable to her. "Get me in bed and I'll roll over for you? 'Here's the land. It's all Jack's.'? Playing people. Playing the odds. The odds were I'd fall for it?"

Then she did something she'd never done before. She struck out physically. She slapped him across his face. And he just stood there. Didn't even try to stop her, or touch where the red imprint of her hand was forming on his skin. He stood absolutely still, his eyes narrowing. She drew back, clutching her hands to her middle, feeling the sting in her palm. "You…you make me sick," she uttered.

"You believe that I did that?" he finally asked in a flat voice.

"Yes, I do. I was right about you from the start."

He shook his head, then moved toward her, but she could have saved herself the effort of stepping back out of his path. He went around her, grabbed his jacket off her sofa and left. The door closed with a quiet click behind him that was even more final than if he'd slammed it. And she was alone. Completely alone.

BY THE TIME Holly walked back to the clinic, Sierra was with Santa, and Annie appeared decidedly green around the gills again. She'd just found out she was pregnant—after years of trying, then finally giving up. She'd found out the day Sierra had gotten sick, but hadn't told Holly that until Sierra was out of danger. Poor Annie. Morning sickness was about to do her in. Rick took her home, hugging her protectively, and the sight of them together tightened something in Holly. She'd let Cain walk with his arm around her, and now he was gone.

Gordie drove the two of them back to her house an hour later and made sure they got settled in. Holly went into Sierra's room with her and stayed with her during her nap. Going into her own bedroom was out of the question for now. She couldn't do it. Not yet. She would, but only when she knew she could see the bed and not be sick. She settled Sierra, then went into the kitchen to make some tea, and was startled by the phone ringing.

She hesitated, then reached for the receiver. She expected Annie to be calling. She feared it might be Cain. But Jack was on the other end. "Holly, do you know where Cain is?"

She held tightly to the receiver. "No, I don't."

"Didn't he say where he was going?"

"Jack, he didn't tell me anything. And the land isn't for sale. Next time you come yourself to get the land. Don't send Cain to do your dirty work."

"Oh, hey, I don't know what you think, but—"

"I think I'm sick of this whole thing," she said, and hung up on him.

The phone had barely hit the base when someone knocked at the door. She stood still, then heard Annie's voice and hurried to open the door for her sister. Annie seemed fine now, and back to her old self. "How's the sickness?" Holly asked.

"Gone for now," she said with a grin as she took off her coat. "I never asked if you got your shopping done?"

Her shopping? She'd totally forgotten about that. Las Vegas seemed a lifetime ago to her now. "Oh, no, that locket. I spent so much time…"

"Well, go do it. I'll sit here with the baby." She touched her perfectly flat stomach. "I could use the practice."

She almost refused, but realized she had to breathe fresh air and get her life back on track. "Okay, I will."

Annie held out her car keys. "Since your car's not around, take mine."

Her car? She'd completely forgotten about it. "Oh, yes, thanks," she said, and got the keys from her, too. She'd have to try to find the mechanic Cain had used to fix it. Which meant she'd have to speak to Cain again. Maybe on the phone that would be doable, she thought, but doubted it.

Ten minutes later, Holly was on the main street of Silver Creek, walking past shops aglow with Christmas lights and filled with decorations. Music was piped out from hidden speakers all around, and people passed, laughing and smiling and happy. She felt distant from the festive air, and it was all she could do to keep walking and not retreat to her house.

Someone bumped her shoulder and she muttered, "Sorry." Then she heard a voice.

"I was heading over to your house in a while."

Jack was in front of her. Jack, bundled in a heavy overcoat, his hands pushed in his pockets. "You."

"Yeah, me. I wasn't going to let our conversation end with you hanging up on me," he said, then motioned to a coffee shop they'd stopped in front of. "How about getting something hot, then talking."

"The land isn't for sale," she said on a weary sigh.

"I know. I know. Believe me."

She frowned at him. "You do?"

"Finally, yes, I do."

"Then why did Cain—"

He shook his head. "Cain didn't. He wouldn't. You might not realize this about him, but he's very straitlaced about some things, and truth is one of them. Oh, like all kids he'd tell small lies, but he'd also get in a pile of trouble when we were kids simply because he told the truth. 'Were you skiing around cars on Main Street?' Josh's dad would ask. I'd stand there like an idiot, and Cain would say, 'Yes, sir. I sure was,' and take his punishment. I never understood that. But that's the way he is."

"You didn't ask him to work on me about the land?"

Jack's expression was a mixture of chagrin and embarrassment. "Yeah, I did, at first. Then he told me that he'd asked and you said, 'No,' and that was that. He meant it. No matter what I said, he didn't relent."

"But I heard him talking to you on the phone about the land."

Jack looked confused, then said, "Oh, yeah, sure, he called to tell me about your little girl, and that he might be sticking around Silver Creek."

That stunned her. "You didn't ask him about the land?"

"Sure I did. But not that land. Not your land. It's land he was in on buying with me and Josh years ago. I wanted to talk to him about buying me out, or Josh buying me out."

"You what?"

"That's it."

"And my land?"

"It's yours. It would be a tremendous asset for the Inn, but I've got other things to think about now."

She felt her head go light for a minute, then horror settled in at what she'd said to Cain. "Where is he?" she asked Jack.

"I don't know. That's what I wanted to talk to you about."

"What about his helicopter?"

"It's at the Inn, waiting for the snow to be cleared."

"Oh, no," she whispered. She'd destroyed everything. Just because she assumed the worst, the absolute worst, and let fear drive her. Even more horribly, she knew in her heart that the Cain she'd made love to was the real Cain. The man she loved with everything she possessed. "I need to…" What? "I need to get back home," she said, then added, "If Cain calls you, would you tell him…? Just tell him I need to see him."

He nodded. "Sure," he said. "But if you see him first, you tell him to call me, okay?"

"I will," she said, and turned to walk back to her car. But when she passed a toy store, the display in the window caused her to stop. She'd come shopping but hadn't known what she was shopping for until then. She went inside, made her purchase, had it wrapped, and put the small box in her jacket pocket, then she left.

She didn't go home. She went to Rusty's Diner, sat in a booth and drank hot chocolate while she stared out the windows at Silver Creek. She'd been wrong about so much. First about Cain, then other things in her life. His words echoed in her mind: *"Does having either thing, the land or the locket change your memories?"* he'd asked. *"Is it that connection with the past? With your parents? You're keeping that alive? If you didn't have either thing, wouldn't you still be Holly?"*

Did the land or the locket make her who she was? Was holding on to the past the way to protect her future, or was it a way to control her future? *"If you didn't have either thing, wouldn't you still be Holly?"* Would keeping the land make her father the father she'd always wanted?

She knew the answers to those questions. Knew she was holding on to all the wrong things and that she'd driven away the one thing that gave her a future—Cain. She'd kept that land hoping that someday she'd feel right about her father. That was foolish. He'd been what he'd been. Period. She'd loved him, faults and all. Keeping the land wouldn't wipe out those faults.

That was a fact, and she'd accept it, just as much as she accepted the fact that she had to reach Cain. She finished her hot chocolate, paid, then left and got in Annie's car and drove home. Annie left a few minutes later, said Sierra had been up and eaten soup and crackers and was asleep again. She was cool and well. When her sister left, Holly went in, checked on Sierra, then went back to the kitchen and reached for the phone.

CAIN DROVE all the way back to Las Vegas in the borrowed car and didn't stop until he was at the Dream Catcher and up in his apartment. He walked in the door and faced the fact that he was alone. It was painful after what he'd almost had. Truly painful. But he knew being alone was his life. He'd always been alone, so things weren't so very different, he told himself. At least, they shouldn't feel that way. Yet they did.

He ignored the ringing phone, letting the call go to the answering service, and strode into his bedroom, where he stripped and showered. Then he dressed and headed down into his world of gamblers, and partying people bent on having fun. But it was different for him. When he looked around this time he spotted the people who were alone, sober and intent on a slot machine or a hand at cards. They moved from table to table or machine to machine. As if they had no place to go, as if they were like him, wandering through the world with no one.

He left the casino, went back up to his penthouse and had taken two steps inside, when he realized he wouldn't be staying. He didn't belong here, either. The sense of this being where he existed was gone. Holly had done that to him. The last blow. He fought away the memories of being with her, of that moment in time when he felt that he belonged right there in her arms. That he'd found his home. He pushed them away any way he could, but they persisted, and he'd had enough of them.

He packed a bag, spoke to his second-in-command about taking over for him for a while, then he walked out of what he'd built. He walked out without looking back, got in the borrowed car and headed north. He'd drop off the car for Jack, tell the helicopter pilot to fly the helicopter back to the city, and he'd keep going. He'd land where he landed, and he'd figure out his life. If he could. He drove up the Strip, and when he got to the corner that led into Old Las Vegas, to the original Strip, he turned left and stopped by the pawnshop he'd found Holly at. One more thing, then he'd be gone.

An hour later, he was on the road north. The drive was a blur of memories and odd sensations. Going home? Partly. Running away? Partly. He'd settle the land issue with Jack, giving his share to Jack and Joshua. They could fight over it. He didn't even remember where the damn land was anymore. He'd do whatever it took to get past Holly and this mess, then he'd cut his losses and move on. Where, he'd figure out when he had to.

He got to the Inn just after dawn and had forgotten it was Christmas morning. Everyone was up and happy, carrying presents, even singing songs at breakfast. The sense of fun wore on him, and he went directly up to Jack's apartment. He found Jack at his desk in the office, sitting forward, his head resting on his arms, and he was sound asleep. Cain coughed and Jack groggily looked up at him. "You're back," he mumbled as he stood and raked his fingers through his hair. "Where did you get to? I was looking all over for you yesterday."

"I brought back your car, and I'm here to sign whatever papers you need to give you and Josh my share of the land."

"What?" Jack asked, coming closer, most definitely awake now.

"It's yours. I don't want it."

"How much?"

"A Christmas present from me to you and Josh."

"Hell, no. It's worth—"

"I don't care."

"It's Holly, isn't it?"

He shook his head. "No, it's me."

"Cain, I talked to Holly. I sort of figured out a few things, but—"

The phone rang, and Jack reached for the extension nearest him. He said, "Hello," listened, then said, "No, no, I was awake."

He watched Jack. "Sure, I remember."

He frowned slightly as the caller kept talking. "What?"

The caller spoke more, then Jack said, "Why?"

He finally said, "No, no, okay. If you're sure."

There was a long pause, then Jack said, "Absolutely. I'll send someone by with the papers tomorrow."

Jack listened again, never taking his eyes off Cain. "I told him. Sure, thanks," he said, then hung up.

He went into the living room and sank onto the couch, combing his hair with his fingers again, before he looked up at Cain. "It's my lucky day," he said, and sat back, his arms spread, resting on the back of the couch. "Two big deals. Christmas really did come for me."

"What are you talking about?"

"That was Holly on the phone. She wants to sell me the mountain. She's decided that she doesn't want to keep it."

Cain didn't understand. "Why?"

"I asked, and she didn't say, just that she wants to do it as soon as possible."

That didn't make sense. "She didn't say anything's wrong with Sierra, did she?" Cain asked, suddenly fearful the child might have taken ill again.

"No, and I could hear a child laughing in the background."

Cain released the breath he hadn't known he'd been holding. "Can I keep that car for a while? There're a few things I need to do. I'll bring it back, or have it driven back." He spoke as he was walking toward the outer room.

"Sure, but where are you going?" Jack called after him.

"I have to drop off something," he said as he got to the elevator and hit the down button.

"Cain?" He stepped into the car and looked at Jack. "You aren't coming back, are you?"

Cain shook his head. "No, but I'll be in touch."

The door slid shut, and Cain rode down to the main level, then went out the side door and over to his borrowed car. He had one thing he drop off with Gordie, then he was leaving.

HOLLY STARED OUT the windows of her house. Annie and Rick were playing with a music box that Sierra had received from Santa, and they were singing along, clapping hands, having a good time. She was the one who didn't feel at all festive. She was thrilled that Sierra was fine now, that Annie and Rick were expecting, despite the miserable morning sickness that came on at any time of the day without warning. She was actually relieved that she'd decided to let go of the mountain. But beyond that, she felt restless and unsettled.

"Holly, let's go to the hotel and get the others gifts that Santa left there for Sierra, okay?"

Sierra jumped up, the picture of health. "Oh, Santa!" she squealed.

Holly got her daughter dressed, and when they were ready to leave, she spoke to Annie. "Take her with you in the car. I want to walk."

"Are you sure?" Annie asked.

"Yeah, I'm sure."

Annie gave her a hug, then smiled at her. "I hope you know we aren't going to wait to open the gifts until you get there."

"I didn't think you would," she said, her own smile tight and she knew it.

Annie and Rick left with Sierra. Holly locked up, then went out. Their car was disappearing down the street, its turn signal flashing left, by the time she'd started to go down the steps. She trudged, chin tucked into her jacket collar, to the sidewalk, then made her way onto the partially cleared road and walked down to the main street.

Snow. Cold. Befitting the Christmas season, except for the heaviness in her heart. All her calls to Cain had gone unanswered. She hunched more into the growing wind and neared the school. She kept going and glanced at the clinic. She saw a car there, one she recognized vaguely. She thought it looked like the car Cain had borrowed at the Inn when they'd flown in. It idled near the side door, a cloud of exhaust coming out the tailpipe.

Then the door opened and she thought she was imagining things. Cain was there. Cain, without a hat, wearing his dark leather jacket, turning from the car. He spotted her, and for a moment she thought he'd just go into the clinic. She wasn't sure what she would have done if he had. She stood very still, waiting, and he finally lifted a hand in her direction, then walked through the snow toward her.

"Holly," he said as he got nearer, and his voice seemed to echo around her.

He was close, but the distance between them could have been a mile. He was removed in some way, was holding himself back, and she could feel it acutely. "What are you doing here?"

"Taking care of something," he said vaguely. "How about you?"

"Walking to the hotel. It seems Santa left some presents there for Sierra."

"You're selling Jack the mountain," he said.

"Yes, I am."

"Why?" he asked, his eyes narrowing on her.

Her breath tightened in her chest, and she made herself speak calmly. "I thought about it, and realized I was holding on to it for all the wrong reasons. I'm letting go of it and the memories. I can't make them any better. I never had a real dad, not any more than the other things in my life were real. Sierra's real. That's all that counts, and the mountain is worth enough to give Sierra what she needs in this life." Holly took a breath. "And you were right. That land doesn't define me. It never did."

"Boy, you figured out a lot, didn't you?" he murmured.

"Some, but—" She bit her lip.

"I was going to let you know that Mike will deliver your car tomorrow. He's got your phone number and your address. He'll have it in Silver Creek by the afternoon."

"Thanks," she said. "Why are you here?"

"I had one last thing to do. I was going to ask Gordie to do it for me, but since you're here, I think I'll do it myself." He pulled his hand out of his pocket and had a tiny box with a slender ribbon on it. "Here."

She didn't move to take it. "No, no," she said, shaking her head. "I don't want a gift."

"I don't buy Christmas presents. I never have. This is yours," he said in a low voice, and reached out to hold her hand with his, then put the box in the center of her palm. "Some memories are worth holding on to." She closed her hand around the box, then glanced down at it. The foil wrapping paper sparkled in the sunlight. She glanced at Cain, and he nodded. "Open it."

She did, her fingers not quite steady around the black velvet box. She gasped when she saw her locket lying on the plush material. Her mother's locket. "How…?"

"I knew you wanted it, and I persuaded the pawnshop owner to part with it last night."

"Why did you do that?" she asked, her hand closing around the small velvet box. "Why?"

He looked almost pained at her question, then he took a breath. "Because…" He shrugged. "I want you to be happy, no matter what you think of me, or what you think I've done, or what you think I am."

His words cut into her heart, and she could barely breathe. "Oh, Cain," she said, her words tremulous on her lips. "I was so wrong. I mean, really wrong. I'm sorry. That's why I've been calling you. I needed to apologize for what I said."

"You know," he said in a low voice, "the closest I've ever come to family is Jack and Josh, maybe Gordie. And I'd do anything for any of them. Anything. But I never would have played you to get some piece of land. I never would have slept with you to get the land."

"Then why did you?" she asked.

He was silent for a long, agonizing moment, then he said, "I'm a gambler, Holly, and that was my biggest gamble. I did it because I love you." He seemed uncertain, with that vulnerability she'd thought she'd seen in him before.

In that moment truth fell on truth. She knew with a certainty that Cain was as far removed from Travis's treachery and her father's indifference as night was from day. She'd been wrong about a lot of things, but she hadn't been wrong about her love for Cain Stone. She put the locket in her pocket and felt something there. Her fingers curled around it and she pulled it out. "Here," she said, remembering. "It's for you." He looked down at a small rectangular wooden box in her hand. She held it out to him. "My present to you. I do give Christmas gifts."

He stared at it, then back at her. "Did you hear what I said?" he asked.

She nodded, then took his hand, turned it palm up and put the wooden box in it. "Please, open it."

He hesitated, uncertainty in his eyes, then he opened the box. He flashed a glance back at Holly, then removed a simple silver harmonica from the box. "It's yours as long as you agree to say it came from Santa, if anyone asks where you got it."

He laughed, but the sound was as unsteady as she felt. "Okay, why did you get it for me?" he asked.

She looked him in the eye and spoke the naked truth. "Because I hated the idea of a little boy who stopped believing in Santa because he never got what he asked for."

"And?" he said softly, the uncertainty in his eyes fading.

"And I love that little boy and the man he's become."

Cain hugged her to him, and then he kissed her, and what had been cold and unbearable up to then became wondrous and glorious. Cain was home. He'd finally figured out where he belonged, and it was right here with Holly. "I love you," he whispered against her lips, and the world fell into place for him. "Stay with me? Be with me? Don't leave me?"

"Oh, I think you've won again," she told him. "Your lucky streak is intact. I'll never leave you." Then she buried her face in his chest. "Merry, Merry Christmas, Cain," she said, her voice muffled against his heart.

"Yes, Merry Christmas," he echoed, and kissed her again.

Epilogue

Cain wasn't quite certain why Annie and Rick hadn't been surprised to see him show up with Holly, or surprised when Holly and he had left together later that evening. Annie had simply said, "Have fun," and then gone back to building blocks with Sierra. Rick had nodded to them, smiled slightly and said, "Next Christmas we're really going to have a big family here." His eyes held Cain's. "I like that."

Cain hadn't taken the time to figure it all out, any more than he'd taken the time to figure out how a man who had never wanted or needed anyone, who'd never had a family, suddenly seemed to be in the middle of one. He hurried with Holly out to his car, and they drove in silence back to the Inn, holding hands to keep the connection that he desperately never wanted to sever. They only let go when they had to get out of the car. Then he was around by her, gathering her to him, lifting her high in his arms and carrying her into the luxurious cabin.

No words were needed as they stood in the silence, holding each other, slowly taking off each other's clothing, then going into the bedroom, falling into the huge poster bed and turning to each other. The shadows were deep, but Cain could see Holly, the outline of her naked hip, the curve of her shoulder. He felt her hands on him and he found her with his hands.

They touched and explored, kissed and stroked, until neither one could stand the separation any longer.

Then she came to him. It was that simple and that complex. Holly came to him. And he welcomed her with all his heart. He entered her and filled her, the way she was filling his life, spreading into the dark, lonely corners of his soul and giving him peace. He loved her completely, and they were together completely. Then he held her, and he knew that if it were possible, he'd never leave the cabin. He'd never let her go for a second.

He felt her lips press to his naked chest, then she lifted on one arm, her hair tangled around her face, and she slowly touched his chin. Her fingers were unsteady, but even in the low light, he knew there was a smile on her face. "Who would have thought that this could happen?" she said to him.

He chuckled, but the sound was rough and slightly breathless in his own ears. "Not me," he admitted with naked honesty.

She kissed him, a long, lingering caress, then drew back with a husky sigh. "Me, neither."

He pulled her down on his chest and buried his face in her fragrant hair. He closed his eyes tightly. "I'm new at all of this," he admitted softly. "I'm new at loving anyone."

When she spoke, the heat of her breath brushed his skin. "You're doing so very well at it. You're a natural."

He doubted that, but she made it so easy to love her and love her daughter. "I'm going to go slow with Sierra. I don't want her to think I'm trying to take her father's place."

That brought tension to Holly. He could feel it in the way her hand stilled on his stomach. She lifted her head, looking at him from mere inches away. "Oh, Cain, don't even think like that. Travis is her father biologically, but he's never been there for her. Not the way you were when she was sick."

"I wanted to make it all right," he breathed. "I couldn't stand to see you so afraid and her so sick."

When Holly spoke her voice was unsteady. "And I couldn't stand to see you so alone. That's why I got you the harmonica. I needed you to realize that dreams do come true—at least, some dreams do."

He let the fact that he wasn't alone anymore sink into his soul, and it felt good. Dreams did come true. He wouldn't figure the odds of that happening, he'd just accept that it had happened to him. He tangled his fingers in her hair, brought her close to kiss her, then said, "You know, I think I'll learn to play the harmonica."

She drew back with mock shock. "You don't even know how to play the thing?"

"Well, I'm willing to learn," he murmured, his left hand stroking her shoulder, then going lower to rest on her hip. "I'm a very fast learner, and since you're a teacher…" His hand came around to her stomach, then back up toward her breast. As he found her breast, he felt her breath catch. "I'm more then willing to let you boss me around and teach me anything you want to teach me."

Her hand moved then, onto his stomach, then lower, until he was the one to gasp in the shadows. "If you're willing to take the gamble, I'm more then willing to teach you anything you want…forever," she whispered, then came to him. "Welcome home, Cain Stone."

The gambler wasn't gambling this time. He knew. This was a sure thing. Holly and Sierra and him. A very sure thing. Home. The place he'd run from had been the very place he'd been looking for all his life. No, the place where the other part of his soul had been waiting for him. That was home. Holly was home for him. "Thank you," he breathed, and knew, too, that he'd never meant anything more in his life.

It's time for some BLOND JUSTICE! This is Kara Lennox's third book in her trilogy about three women who were duped by the same con man. Sonya Patterson's mother has been busy preparing her daughter's wedding—and has no idea the groom-to-be ran off with Sonya's money. Will the blondes finally get their sweet revenge on the evil Marvin? And how long can Sonya pretend that she's going through with the wedding—when she'd rather be married to her long-time bodyguard, John-Michael McPhee? We know you're going to love this funny, fast-paced story!

Airplane seats were way too small, and too crowded together. Sonya Patterson had never thought much about this before, since she'd always flown first class in the past. But this was a last-minute ticket on a no-first-class kind of plane.

She'd also never flown on a commercial airline with her bodyguard, which might explain her current claustrophobia. John-Michael McPhee was a broad-shouldered, well-muscled man, and Sonya was squashed between him and a hyperactive seven-year-old whose mother was fast asleep in the row behind them.

She could smell the leather of McPhee's bomber jacket. He'd had that jacket for years, and every time Sonya saw him in it, her stupid heart gave a little leap. She hated herself for letting him affect her that way. Didn't most women get over their teenage crushes by the time they were pushing thirty?

"I didn't know you were a nervous flier," McPhee said, brushing his index finger over her left hand. Sonya realized she was clutching her armrests as if the plane were about to crash.

What would he think, she wondered, if she blurted out that it wasn't flying that made her nervous, it was being so close to him? Her mother would not approve of Sonya's messy feelings where McPhee was concerned.

Her mother. Sonya's heart ached at the thought of her vibrant mother lying in a hospital bed hooked up to machines. Muffy Lockridge Patterson was one of those women who never stopped, running all day, every day at full throttle with a To-Do list a mile long. Over the years, Sonya had often encouraged her mother to slow down, relax and cut back on the rich foods. But Muffy seldom took advice from anyone.

Sonya consciously loosened her grip on the armrests when McPhee nudged her again.

"She'll be okay," he said softly. "She was in stable condition when I left."

A comfortable silence passed before McPhee asked, "Are you going to tell me what you were doing in New Orleans with your 'sorority sister'?"

So, he hadn't bought her cover story. But she'd had to come up with something quickly when McPhee had tracked her down hundreds of miles away from where she was supposed to be. She'd already been caught in a bald-faced lie— for weeks she'd been telling her mother she was at a spa in Dallas, working out her pre-wedding jitters.

"I was just having a little fun," she tried again.

"A little fun that got you in trouble with the FBI?"

This is the first book in an exciting new miniseries from Jacqueline Diamond, DOWNHOME DOCTORS. The town of Downhome, Tennessee, has trouble keeping doctors at its small clinic. Advertising an available position at the town's clinic brings more than one candidate for the job, but the townspeople get more than they bargained for when Dr. Jenni Vine is hired, despite Police Chief Ethan Forrest's reservations about her—at least in the beginning!

"Nobody knows better than I do how badly this town needs a doctor," Police Chief Ethan Forrest told the crowd crammed into the Downhome, Tennessee, city council chambers. "But please, not Jenni Vine."

He hadn't meant to couch his objection so bluntly, he mused as he registered the startled reaction of his audience. Six months ago, he'd been so alarmed by the abrupt departure of the town's two resident doctors, a married couple, that he'd probably have said yes to anyone with an M.D. after his or her name.

Worried about his five-year-old son, Nick, who was diabetic, Ethan had suggested that the town advertise for physicians to fill the vacated positions. They'd also recommended that they hire a long-needed obstetrician.

Applications hadn't exactly poured in. Only two had arrived from qualified family doctors, both of whom had toured Downhome recently by invitation. One was clearly superior, and as a member of the three-person search committee, Ethan felt it his duty to say so.

"Dr. Gregory is more experienced and, in my opinion, more stable. He's married with three kids, and I believe he's motivated to stick around for the long term." Although less than ideal in one respect, the Louisville physician took his duties seriously and, Ethan had no doubt, would fit into the community.

"Of course he's motivated!" declared Olivia Rockwell, who stood beside Ethan just below the city council's dais. The tall African-American woman, who was the school principal, chaired the committee. "You told us yourself he's a recovering alcoholic."

"He volunteered the information, along with the fact that he's been sober for a couple of years," Ethan replied. "His references are excellent and he expressed interest in expanding our public health efforts. I think he'd be perfect to oversee the outreach program I've been advocating."

"So would Jenni—I mean Dr. Vine," said the third committee member, Karen Lowell, director of the Tulip Tree Nursing Home. "She's energetic and enthusiastic. Everybody likes her."

"She certainly has an outgoing personality," he responded. On her visit, the California blonde had dazzled people with her expensive clothes and her good humor after being drenched in a thunderstorm, which she seemed to regard as a freak of nature. It probably didn't rain on her parade very often out there in the land of perpetual sunshine, Ethan supposed. "But once the novelty wears off, she'll head for greener pastures and we'll need another doctor."

"So you aren't convinced she'll stay? Is that the extent of your objections?" Olivia asked. "This isn't typical of you, Chief. I'll bet you've got something else up that tailored sleeve of yours."

Ethan was about to pass off her comment as a joke, when

he noticed some of the townsfolk leaning forward in their seats with anticipation. Despite being a quiet place best known for dairy farmers and a factory that made imitation antiques, Downhome had an appetite for gossip.

Although Ethan had hoped to avoid going into detail, the audience awaited his explanation. Was he being unfair? True, he'd taken a mild dislike to Dr. Vine's surfer-girl demeanor, but he could get over that. What troubled him was the reason she'd wanted to leave L.A. in the first place.

"You all know I conducted background checks on the candidates," he began. "Credit records, convictions, that sort of thing."

"And found no criminal activities, right?" Karen tucked a curly strand of reddish-brown hair behind one ear.

"That's correct. But I also double-checked with the medical directors at their hospitals." He had a bomb to drop now, so he'd better get it over with.

This is the final book of Dianne Castell's FORTY & FABU-LOUS trilogy about three women living in Whistlers Bend, Montana, who are dealing (or not dealing!) with turning forty. Dixie Carmichael has just had her fortieth birthday, and gotten the best birthday present of all—a second chance at life—after the ultimate medical scare. One thing she's sure of—now's the time to start living life the way she's always wanted it to be!

Dixie Carmichael twisted her fingers into the white sheet as she lay perfectly still on the O.R. table and tried to remember to breathe. Fear settled in her belly like sour milk. *She was scared!* Bone-numbing, jelly-legged, full-blown-migraine petrified. It wasn't every day her left breast got turned into a giant pincushion.

She closed her eyes, not wanting to look at the ultrasound machine or think about the biopsy needle or anything else in the overly bright sterile room that would determine if the lump was really bad news.

She clenched her teeth so they wouldn't chatter, then prayed for herself and all women who ever went, or would go, through this. The horror of waiting to find out the diagnosis was more terrifying than her divorce and wrapping her Camaro around a tree rolled into one.

God, let me out of this and I'll change. I swear it. No more pity parties over getting dumped by Danny for that Victoria's Secret model, no more comfort junk food, no more telling everyone how to live their lives and not really living her own, and if that meant leaving Whistlers Bend, she'd suck it up and do it and quit making excuses.

"We're taking out the fluid now," the surgeon said. "It's clear."

Dixie's eyes shot wide open. She swallowed, then finally managed to ask, "Meaning?"

The surgeon stayed focused on what she was doing, but the news was good. Dixie could tell—she'd picked up being able to read people from waiting tables at the Purple Sage restaurant for three years and dealing with happy, way-less-than-happy and everything-in-between customers. *Oh, how she wished she were at the Purple Sage now.*

The surgeon continued. "Meaning the lump in your breast is a cyst. I'll send the fluid we drew off to the pathologist to be certain, but there's no indication the lump was anything more than a nuisance."

Nuisance! A nuisance was a telemarketer, a traffic ticket, gaining five pounds! But the important thing was, she'd escaped. She said another prayer for the women who wouldn't escape. Then she got dressed and left the hospital, resisting the urge to turn handsprings all the way to her car. Or maybe she did them, she wasn't sure.

She could go home. In one hour she'd be back in Whistlers Bend. Her life still belonged to her, and not doctors and hospitals and pills and procedures. She fired up her Camaro and sat for a moment, appreciating the familiar idle of her favorite car while staring out at the flat landscape of Billings, Montana. This was one of the definitive moments when life smacked her upside the head and said, *Dixie, old girl, get your ass in gear.*

You've wanted action, adventure, hair-raising experiences as long as you can remember. Now's the time to make them happen!

Welcome back to Laramie, Texas, and a whole new crop of McCabes! In this story, prankster Riley McCabe is presented with three abandoned children one week before Christmas. Thinking it's a joke played on him by Amanda Witherspoon, he comes to realize the kids really do need his help. Watch out for Cathy Gillen Thacker's next book, *A Texas Wedding Vow,* in April 2006.

Amanda Witherspoon had heard Riley McCabe was returning to Laramie, Texas, to join the Laramie Community Hospital staff, but she hadn't actually *seen* the handsome family physician until Friday afternoon when he stormed into the staff lounge in the pediatrics wing.

Nearly fourteen years had passed, but his impact on her was the same. Just one look into his amber eyes made her pulse race, and her emotions skyrocket. He had been six foot when he left for college, now he was even taller. Back then he had worn his sun-streaked light brown hair any which way. Now the thick wavy strands were cut in a sophisticated fashion, parted neatly on the left and brushed casually to the side. He looked solid and fit, mouthwateringly sexy, and every inch the kind of grown man who knew exactly who he was and what he wanted out of life. The kind not to be messed with. Amanda thought the sound of holiday music playing on the hospital sound system and the Christmas tree in the corner only added to the fantasy-come-true quality of the situation.

Had she not known better, Amanda would have figured Riley McCabe's return to her life would have been the Christmas present to beat all Christmas presents, meant to liven up her increasingly dull and dissatisfying life. But wildly exciting things like that never happened to Amanda.

"Notice I'm not laughing," Riley McCabe growled as he passed close enough for her to inhale the fragrance of soap and brisk, wintry cologne clinging to his skin.

"Notice," Amanda returned dryly, wondering what the famously mischievous prankster was up to now, "neither am I."

Riley marched toward her, jaw thrust out pugnaciously, thick straight brows raised in mute admonition. "I would have figured we were beyond all this."

Amanda had hoped that would be the case, too. After all, she was a registered nurse, he a doctor. But given the fact that the Riley McCabe she recalled had been as full of mischief as the Texas sky was big, that had been a dangerous supposition to make. "Beyond all what?" she repeated around the sudden dryness of her throat. As he neared her, all the air left her lungs in one big whoosh.

"The practical jokes! But you just couldn't resist, could you?"

Amanda put down the sandwich she had yet to take a bite of and took a long sip of her diet soda. "I have no idea what you're talking about," she said coolly. Unless this was the beginning of yet another ploy to get her attention?

"Don't you?" he challenged, causing another shimmer of awareness to sift through her.

Deciding that sitting while he stood over her gave him too much of a physical advantage, she pushed back her chair and rose slowly to her feet. She was keenly aware that he now had a good six inches on her, every one of them as bold and masculine as the set of his lips. "I didn't think you were due to start working here until January," she remarked, a great deal more casually than she felt.

He stood in front of her, arms crossed against his chest, legs braced apart, every inch of him taut and ready for action. "I'm not."

"So?" She ignored the intensity in the long-lashed amber eyes that threatened to throw her off balance. "How could I possibly play a prank on you if I didn't think you were going to be here?"

"Because," he enunciated, "you knew I was going to start setting up my office in the annex today."

Amanda sucked in a breath. "I most certainly did not!" she insisted. Although she might have had she realized he intended to pick up right where they had left off, all those years ago. Matching wits and wills. The one thing she had never wanted to cede to the reckless instigator was victory of any kind.

Riley leaned closer, not stopping until they were practically close enough to kiss. "Listen to me, Amanda, and listen good. Playing innocent is not going to work with me. And neither," he warned, even more forcefully, "is your latest gag."

Amanda regarded him in a devil-may-care way designed to get under his skin as surely as he was already getting under hers. "I repeat," she spoke as if to the village idiot, "I have no idea what you are talking about, Dr. McCabe. Now, do you mind? I only have a forty-five-minute break and I'd like to eat my lunch."

He flashed her an incendiary smile that left her feeling more aware of him than ever. "I'll gladly leave you alone just as soon as you collect them."

Amanda blinked, more confused than ever. "Collect who?" she asked incredulously.

Riley walked back to the door. Swung it open wide. On the other side was the surprise of Amanda's life.

If you enjoyed what you just read,
then we've got an offer you can't resist!

Take 2 bestselling love stories FREE!
Plus get a FREE surprise gift!

Home For The Holidays!

Receive a FREE Christmas Collection
containing 4 books by bestselling authors

**Harlequin American Romance and Silhouette Special Edition
invite you to celebrate Home For The Holidays by offering you this
exclusive offer valid only in Harlequin American Romance and
Silhouette Special Edition books this November.**

To receive your FREE Christmas Collection, send us 3 (three) proofs of
purchase of Harlequin American Romance or Silhouette Special Edition
books to the addresses below.

Home For The Holidays!

While there are many variations of this recipe, here is Tina Leonard's favorite!

GOURMET REINDEER POOP

Mix 1/2 cup butter, 2 cups granulated sugar, 1/2 cup milk and 2 tsp cocoa together in a large saucepan.

Bring to a boil, stirring constantly; boil for 1 minute.

Remove from heat and stir in 1/2 cup peanut butter, 3 cups oatmeal (not instant) and 1/2 cup chopped nuts (optional).

Drop by teaspoon full (larger or smaller as desired) onto wax paper and let harden.

They will set in about 30-60 minutes.

These will keep for several days without refrigerating, up to 2 weeks refrigerated and 2-3 months frozen.

Pack into resealable sandwich bags and attach the following note to each bag.

I woke up with such a scare when I heard Santa call…
"Now dash away, dash away, dash away all!"
I ran to the lawn and in the snowy white drifts,
those nasty reindeer had left "little gifts."
I got an old shovel and started to scoop,
neat little piles of "Reindeer Poop!"
But to throw them away seemed such a waste,
so I saved them, thinking you might like a taste!
As I finished my task, which took quite a while,
Old Santa passed by and he sheepishly smiled.
And I heard him exclaim as he was in the sky…
"Well, they're not potty trained, but at least they can fly!"